Look

Garden Girls
Cozy Mystery Series Book 12
Hope Callaghan

hopecallaghan.com

Copyright © 2016
All rights reserved.

This book is a work of fiction. Although places mentioned may be real, the characters, names and incidents, and all other details are products of the author's imagination and are fictitious. Any resemblance to actual events or actual persons, living or dead is purely coincidental.

No part of this publication may be copied, reproduced in any format, by any means, electronic or otherwise, without prior consent from the copyright owner and publisher of this book. The only exception is brief quotations in printed reviews.

Visit my website for new releases and special offers: hopecallaghan.com

Thank you, Peggy Hyndman, Jean Pilch and Cindi Graham for taking the time to preview *Look Into My Ice,* for the extra sets of eyes and for catching all my mistakes.

Table of Contents

Get Free Books and More! iv

Meet the Author v

Foreword.. vi

Chapter 1.. 1

Chapter 2.. 12

Chapter 3.. 25

Chapter 4.. 38

Chapter 5.. 50

Chapter 6.. 59

Chapter 7.. 71

Chapter 8.. 84

Chapter 9.. 98

Chapter 10.. 110

Chapter 11.. 118

Chapter 12.. 127

Chapter 13.. 136

Chapter 14.. 143

Chapter 15.. 156

Chapter 16.. 171

Chapter 17.. 183

Chapter 18... 197
Chapter 19... 211
Chapter 20... 229
Chapter 21... 243
"Stick to your ribs" Goulash 263

Get Free Books and More!

Sign up for my Free Cozy Mysteries Newsletter to get free and discounted books, giveaways & soon-to-be-released books!

hopecallaghan.com/newsletter/

Meet the Author

Hope Callaghan is an author who loves to write Christian books, especially Christian Mystery and Cozy Mystery books. She has written more than 30 mystery books (and counting) in four series.

Born and raised in a small town in West Michigan, she now lives in Florida with her husband.

She is the proud mother of one daughter and a stepdaughter and stepson. When she's not doing the thing she loves best - writing books - she enjoys cooking, traveling and reading books.

Hope loves to connect with her readers! Connect with her today!

Visit hopecallaghan.com for special offers, free books, and soon-to-be-released books!

Email: hope@hopecallaghan.com

Facebook page: https://www.facebook.com/hopecallaghanauthor/

Foreword

Dear Reader,

I would like to personally thank you for purchasing this book and also to let you know that a portion of all my book sales go to support missions which proclaim the Good News of Jesus Christ.

My prayer is that you will be blessed by reading my stories and knowing that you are helping to spread the Gospel of the Lord.

With more than thirty mystery books (and counting) in four series published, I hope you will have as much fun reading them as I have writing them!

May God Bless You!

Sincerely,

Author Hope Callaghan

This Page Intentionally Left Blank

Chapter 1

Gloria Rutherford-Kennedy glared at the pink cast on her left leg and then frowned at the ringing phone. "Stupid cast!"

Gloria had broken her leg a few weeks earlier while on her honeymoon. She had fallen into a gopher tortoise hole while chasing a peeping tom on her sister, Liz's, camper lot.

The cast was making her cranky and cramping her style. She was counting the days until the cast would come off and it wasn't going to be one moment too soon!

Gloria hobbled to the house phone. "Hello?"

"Gloria?" Gloria had to press the phone close to her ear to hear the soft voice on the other end of the line.

The female voice was familiar but for the life of her, Gloria couldn't place it, at least not right off the bat.

"This is Eleanor Whittaker. I was wondering if you had a moment to stop by my place this morning."

Gloria could count on one hand the number of times Eleanor had called to ask something of Gloria. Whatever she wanted must be important, or perhaps Eleanor was ill. "Is everything alright, Eleanor?"

"Yes. I-I'm fine, but I have something that may be of interest to you, and wondered if you might have time to stop by. This morning."

Gloria glanced out the window. It was mid-February. West Michigan was smack-dab in the middle of a "January thaw." The thick layer of snow that had blanketed the ground and area roads had melted, making everything a soupy mess.

The warmer weather wasn't going to last long. Forecasters were predicting a doozy of a storm that was barreling across the plains and headed right toward Michigan.

Gloria wasn't complaining about the warmer weather. She was happy she wouldn't have to maneuver along the snow-covered sidewalks and driveways while attempting to balance on her one good foot.

"You want me to come by now?" It wasn't that Gloria had anything pressing to take care of, but she hadn't planned to leave the farm.

"Yes. As soon as you are able."

Paul, Gloria's husband, had taken on a side job working as security for a presidential hopeful who was in town campaigning. He had left before sunrise and said he would be back in time for dinner.

Gloria had spent the morning puttering around the house, combing through her closets in an attempt to find warm weather outfits to pack for the upcoming cruise with her friends, the Garden Girls.

Since returning from her honeymoon, the days had been filled with not only catching up with her friends, but also visiting the shut-ins in the area, delivering baked goods and keeping them company. Eleanor was one of them.

Paul and she had also been trying to sort through some of their things to try to clear the clutter, all the while dealing with the dreaded cast.

Eleanor lowered her voice, as if someone might be listening in. "Something is going on down at the lake!" The lake being, Lake Terrace. Eleanor's home was perched on a hill overlooking the lake.

Gloria was all ears now. "Has someone fallen through the ice?"

Despite the "January thaw," the lake was still frozen solid and a good number of shanties dotted the lake. In fact, the ice was so thick; some of the men drove their snowmobiles and even their pick-up trucks onto the lake and parked right next to their shanties.

"Well..." Eleanor's voice trailed off. "You'll have to come see for yourself."

Eleanor loved to have the Garden Girls stop by for Sunday visits. She was always eager to find out if there were any new investigations under way and had tried to help the girls on several occasions with tidbits of information.

So far, all of Eleanor's leads had been dead ends. There was only one way to find out if this one would be the same. "I'm on my way."

Gloria disconnected the line, limped to the door, slipped into her winter jacket, and then dropped her purse over her neck before grabbing her keys off the hook near the door.

Mally, Gloria's beloved springer spaniel, met her at the door.

"I'm going to Eleanor's place. You want to go see Eleanor?" Eleanor loved Mally and always had treats waiting when they arrived for a visit.

Mally thumped her tail against the door and let out a low whine.

Gloria opened the door and waited for Mally to trot out onto the porch before closing the door behind them.

She hobbled to the garage, opened the side service door and then the rear door of her car, a 1989 Mercury Grand Marquis she had nicknamed Annabelle many moons ago.

While Gloria scooched behind the wheel, grumbling about her troublesome cast the entire time, Mally settled into the backseat.

It was only a couple miles from Gloria's farm to the small town of Belhaven. When she reached the main drag, she turned right at the stop sign and headed toward Lake Terrace and Eleanor's home on the hill.

Eleanor had given up driving a couple years back after a harrowing incident. She had gotten confused, accidentally accelerated instead of hitting the brakes and had plowed her caddy into the corner of the Quik Stop, Belhaven's grocery store.

It had scared the dickens out of Sally Keane, who had been working behind the cash register. Sally managed to scramble across the checkout counter to safety, narrowly escaping significant bodily harm.

Sally had cleared the counter, barely grazed by the caddy's bumper but to hear her re-enactment, Eleanor had nearly killed her and had even hinted that poor Eleanor had spotted Sally and decided to take her out by hitting the gas instead of the brake.

Gloria turned into the circular drive and stopped in front of the porch steps. She held the door for Mally, who vaulted out of the back seat and darted up the steps, waiting for Gloria near the front door.

She was halfway across the drive when the door swung open.

Eleanor stood in the doorway wringing her hands, an anxious expression painted on her face. "Thank you for coming so fast, Gloria. I just know something is going on down by the lake."

Gloria and Mally followed Eleanor and her walker across the living room, through the dining room, past the kitchen and into the family room that overlooked the lake.

They stopped in front of the sliding glass doors.

Eleanor handed Gloria a pair of binoculars. "Here, take a look. There, on the right."

Gloria pressed the binoculars to her eyes and scanned the horizon. Several snowmobiles and a group of people circled one of the fish shanties sitting out on the ice and not far from the shoreline. "That's odd."

Many of the area residents were retirees. The regulars who fished almost daily met out on the lake early in the morning and then headed over to Dot's Restaurant for breakfast so they could brag about their catches.

Gloria shifted on her crutches, adjusted the dial on the binoculars and zoomed in on the shanty. She wasn't keen on fishing, and especially ice fishing, but Paul loved to go out on his days off and had taken his own shanty onto the ice.

The men marked their shanties with their last name, although it wasn't necessary since no one ever messed with someone else's shanty.

She squinted her eyes to read the name on the side.

"Mueller." She lowered the binoculars. The shanty belonged to Ed Mueller. The Mueller family owned a summer cottage on the lake and the cottage was not far from where the shanty was located. Ed worked for Kent County as a meter reader and lived in Grand Rapids with his wife, Sheryl, a middle school math teacher.

Ed and his wife rarely visited the cottage during the winter months and it had been years since he'd gone ice fishing.

"I wonder why Ed's shanty is on the lake."

Eleanor's blue eyes gleamed. "I heard Ed's sister, Fay, died last month down in Indiana and Ed was thinking about selling the cottage."

Gloria set the binoculars on the end table. "I'm gonna go down and check it out."

Eleanor patted Mally's head. "Do you mind if I go with you?"

"Of course not."

On the way to the front door, Eleanor plucked a doggie treat from the container she kept in the kitchen panty and held it out for Mally, who clamped it in her jaw and trotted to the door.

It took several moments for Gloria to make the trek down the steps as she held onto the handrail with one hand and her crutches with the other.

Eleanor was just as cautious as she slowly made her way down the steps and to the passenger side of the car.

Gloria waited for Mally to climb in the back before placing the crutches on the back seat and hobbling to the driver's side door.

Eleanor placed her walker in the back seat and then slid into the front seat. After she had buckled her seatbelt, Gloria drove out of the driveway and headed down the hill toward the lake.

She pulled Annabelle into Ed Mueller's empty driveway and the women, along with Mally, made their way across the drive, the mushy yard and onto the lake.

Eleanor had an easier time navigating the ice as she clung to her walker and slowly inched forward.

The rubber tips of Gloria's crutches were akin to ice skates and she quickly regretted her decision to step out onto the smooth, treacherous ice.

Someone reached out from behind her and grabbed her elbow, steadying her. "What in the world are you doing out here?"

Gloria shot a quick glance to the side. It was Gloria's young friend, Andrea Malone. "Thank heavens. Can you help me get to the shanty?"

"Against my better judgment," Andrea quipped as she continued to hold Gloria's arm and they moved forward at a snail's pace.

Eleanor was already near the shanty and had joined the growing group of spectators.

Whoop...Whoop.

The sound of a police siren sounded behind her and Gloria glanced back. They would need to pick up the pace if they were going to be able to see what was going on before the police arrived on the scene and made everyone leave the vicinity.

Finally, they reached the outer fringes of the people who had gathered.

"What's going on?" Gloria asked of no one in particular.

Glen Shenk, one of the locals who liked to ice fish on the lake, turned to Gloria. "It's Ed Mueller. Looks like he's partially frozen inside the ice!"

Chapter 2

Gloria, accompanied by Andrea, muscled her way through the crowd with a little help from one of her crutches.

They reached the inner circle and Gloria gazed inside the open door. All she could see was Ed's head. Someone had covered his body with a flannel blanket.

"You don't want to look underneath," a man standing next to Gloria remarked.

Glen Shenk followed them to the doorway. "Ed's wife, Sheryl, called down to Dot's Restaurant early this morning, looking for Ed."

Glen continued. "We..." he pointed to Carl Arnett, another one of the Belhaven locals, "offered to run by the cottage to take a look. When we got here, we saw his shanty out on the lake. Guess we never noticed it earlier. Course it was dark and our shanties are on the other side of the lake."

Carl Arnett interrupted. "We knew right then something was wrong. Ed hasn't put his shanty out on the lake for years. We knocked on the cottage door, but no one answered so we came out here and found him."

Carl pointed inside. "We covered him up, trying not to touch anything but it ain't pretty."

Gloria's stomach grew queasy as she gazed at the cold, gray face of Ed Mueller. Had poor Ed, depressed over his sister's recent passing, decided to kill himself? What a tragic way to end one's life. She shifted her gaze to Andrea. "Do you have your cell phone on you?"

Andrea nodded and plucked it from her pocket.

"Take a couple quick pictures," she said in a low voice.

Andrea glanced over her shoulder. Officer Joe Nelson was bearing down on the cluster of gawkers.

"Hurry," Gloria urged.

Andrea turned the phone on, pointed it at the inside of the shanty and tapped the screen.

"Okay folks. Back up." Officer Joe Nelson approached the group of onlookers and began waving his hands.

Andrea slipped the camera into her jacket pocket.

Gloria took a step back and gazed around. Farther out on the water there were several shanties lined up in a row, while still others were set up in semi-circles.

Ed Mueller's shanty was off by itself and close to shore. There were tracks leading from the shanty to the shoreline and into the yard.

Ed would have had to use his pick-up truck to push the shanty onto the lake. Where was his truck?

Officer Derek Jones, another of Montbay County Sheriff's officers, tapped Gloria on the shoulder. "You're gonna have to leave, Gloria."

"I..." Gloria started to answer.

Officer Jones, who had also worked with Gloria's husband, Paul, raised both hands. "You know I would let you hang around if I could, but if I let you then the rest would think I'm showing preferential treatment."

Gloria took one last longing glance inside the shanty and, with Andrea's help, slowly made her way to the shoreline.

Eleanor and Mally were already on shore and stood off to the side while they waited for Andrea and Gloria to catch up.

Eleanor fell in step with Gloria as they made their way across the Mueller's yard toward the car. "I saw a light inside the cottage last night," Eleanor said.

Gloria came to an abrupt halt near the cottage's side door. She glanced at the officers, who stood guard in front of the shanty door. They had told her to leave the ice. There was no mention of the cottage.

Andrea recognized the look in Gloria's eyes. "I don't think..."

It was too late. Gloria adjusted her crutches and hopped to Mueller's cabin door. She lifted the end of her crutch and pressed on the door with the rubber tip. The door creaked open.

Gloria, followed closely by Eleanor, stepped inside the cottage.

A reluctant Andrea, along with Mally, brought up the rear.

The inside of the small cottage was dark, all of the curtains drawn tightly shut.

The pungent odor of mothballs, mixed with a musty smell, filled the air. If Ed Mueller had stayed in the cottage, it hadn't been for a very long time.

Beyond the entrance was a large room. Off in the corner was the kitchen, the decor right out of the 1970's, complete with gold-flecked Formica counters and wooden barn door cabinets.

Rustic iron latches framed the front of the wooden cabinets. With a good cleaning and a coat of stain, the cabinets would look like new.

Sitting on top of the counter was a bag from the hardware store. Gloria peeked inside the bag and spotted a new, unopened door lockset. Under the bag was a "For Sale" sign with the handwritten words "Shanty for Sale," along with a telephone number.

Gloria shuffled out of the kitchen and over to a door, which led to a wood paneled bathroom. The bathroom was decorated in the same rustic charm as the main living area.

She shifted her gaze past the kitchen and into the living room. A wood burning stove sat in the corner. Next to the woodstove was a narrow cot and on top of the cot a sleeping bag.

Gloria hobbled over to the woodstove and placed her hand on top. It was cool to the touch. Even with the warmer temperatures, there was no way anyone could comfortably sleep inside the cottage without heat.

On her way back to the side door, she passed by a small bedroom. The furnishings inside the room were sparse. There was a twin bed on one wall and bunk beds on the opposite wall. A small wooden dresser separated the two. Directly above the dresser was a small window.

Gloria hobbled over to the window, flipped the latch and unlocked the window.

"I thought you left."

Gloria spun around, clutching her crutches and her chest. It was Officer Joe Nelson. "Oh my gosh! You're gonna give an old woman a heart attack!"

The officer grunted. "Old my foot. Your ticker is probably in better shape than mine."

"Maybe if you would lay off the donuts," Gloria teased as she shifted past him and made her way back into the living room.

Andrea, Eleanor and Mally stood near the door.

Gloria limped over to stand next to them and turned back to face the police officer. "What happened to Ed?"

The cop lifted his hat and scratched his forehead. "You know I can't divulge any information, Gloria. We're waiting for a special team to get here so they can break through the ice and retrieve the body."

He nodded toward the bedroom Gloria had just left. "You find anything? I know you were snooping around."

"We weren't snooping," Eleanor insisted. "The door was ajar and we wanted to make sure the place was locked up so no one would get in here."

"So that's why you were inside?" Officer Joe Nelson didn't buy the explanation for one second.

Eleanor stiffened her back. "It's our civic duty to be aware of activity in the area and keep our small town safe."

"All right, Eleanor. Whatever you say." Officer Joe Nelson herded them out of the cottage and closed the door behind him. "This cottage is officially off limits."

He turned his attention to Eleanor. "You have a bird's-eye view of this place, Eleanor. You see anything unusual?"

"Well, I did notice lights on down here by the lake last night," she admitted.

"Do you remember what time?"

She shook her head. "I'm not sure. I'll have to think about it."

Officer Joe Nelson walked the trio and Mally back to the car. It was a nice gesture, but Gloria had a sneaky suspicion it had more to do with him wanting to make sure they had actually left the premises and weren't hanging around.

"Mind if I hitch a ride home?" Andrea asked.

Gloria opened the driver's side door and slipped the crutches over the headrest. "Of course. How did you get here?"

"I walked down. I was out in the backyard with Brutus when I noticed a string of cars heading down the hill toward the lake, so I ran out to the road to see what was happening and saw all the people gathered out on the lake. When I saw your car, I knew something was going on."

Andrea hopped into the back seat and reached for her seat belt as Mally settled in next to her. "How did you know something was going on?"

Gloria started the car and backed out of the drive. "Eleanor tipped me off. She said there was something going on down by the lake so I drove to her place to see what was happening."

"Good eye, Eleanor," Andrea said.

Eleanor smiled. "Ain't got much else to do except watch the goings on from my windows."

She snapped her fingers. "I remember what time I saw the lights down at Ed Mueller's place. I had just eaten dinner and was getting ready to watch Gastronomical Guesses, you know, that new show where they blindfold contestants and then make them guess as many of the ingredients in a dish as possible."

Gloria had briefly watched the show and been intrigued, but ever since Paul and she had returned from their honeymoon, they had been busy. They barely had time to sit down to watch the evening news, let alone a television show. "Go on."

"Well, the contestants were trying a new ice cream dish. It had caramel corn and potato chips, which got me to craving a little ice cream so I headed to the fridge. That's when I saw the lights."

Gloria tapped the steering wheel with the tip of her finger. "So you think it was around 7:30 p.m.?"

"Yep." Eleanor nodded. "Probably closer to 7:45 since they were already on the second round of tasting. The first taste test was pizza made with salsa and topped with raisins."

"Gross," Andrea said. "I bet Alice would like that combination." Alice was Andrea's former housekeeper and her housemate. The woman had a flair for the spicy. In fact, she loved everything with heat...the hotter, the better.

When they reached the stop sign at the top of the hill, Gloria pressed her foot on the brake and looked both ways. "Do you have time to stop by Dot's Restaurant?" she asked both Eleanor and Andrea. "We can put our heads together and discuss the case."

Dot's Restaurant was on Main Street in downtown Belhaven. Dot was Dot Jenkins, one of Gloria's close friends.

Eleanor blinked her eyes behind her wire-rimmed glasses. "You mean I get to be part of the investigation?"

Gloria reached over and patted her hand. "Yes, Eleanor. I believe you will be most helpful sorting out the clues."

Not only that, Eleanor had an unobstructed view of the Mueller cottage and Gloria planned to have her keep it under surveillance until they could figure out what had happened to poor Ed Mueller.

Dot's Restaurant was busy and Gloria guessed it was because of the buzz about Ed's body. News of Ed Mueller's death had probably spread like wildfire and the residents had gathered at the town's unofficial meeting spot – Dot's.

There were no empty spots out front so Gloria had to park across the street in the post office parking lot. The post office was the second busiest place in Belhaven.

Gloria glanced in the front picture window and spied her friend, Ruth, leaning over the counter talking to Judith Arnett.

Judith's husband, Carl, had also been at the shanty and without a doubt, Ruth was pumping Judith for information.

Gloria caught Ruth's eye through the front picture window and Ruth waved frantically for her to come inside.

"I'll catch up with you over at Dot's," she told Andrea and Eleanor as Mally and she made their way into the post office lobby.

"You heard about Ed Mueller?" Ruth blurted out when Gloria stepped inside. "They found Ed's truck over on the other side of the lake, parked in the public access."

"Yeah. Eleanor called this morning to tell me something was going on."

A local resident stepped into the post office and over to the mailboxes. The women waited silently for the person to pull their mail from the slot, sort through the pile and then exit the post office.

Ruth waited for the door to close. "Judith was just telling me Carl saw Officer Joe Nelson talking to Ed Mueller last night out near the Quik Stop. They looked like they were about to start throwing punches."

Chapter 3

Gloria shifted her crutches. "Really?" That meant Ed Mueller *had* been in Belhaven the previous night. Carl and Al Dickerson hadn't mentioned it out on the lake. Of course, it had been chaotic and Gloria hadn't had much of a chance to talk to either of them.

She remembered the cold wood stove and the musty smell inside the cottage. If Ed Mueller had stayed at the cottage the night before, perhaps he had been trying to keep it a secret.

Ruth interrupted Gloria's musings. "I see Eleanor Whittaker is with you. Has she been able to shed any light on the situation?"

Gloria's eyes slid to Judith, who eagerly leaned forward. Judith had a reputation as a blabbermouth and Gloria wondered if what she might share with the women would hit the streets of town. She sucked in a breath. "Eleanor saw a light on at the cottage last night."

It was the truth. That was all they'd had time to discuss. Gloria hoped Eleanor had more information but just hadn't remembered it yet.

Ruth glanced at the clock. "I'm stuck here for another couple of hours," she moaned. "Don't start the investigation without me."

Gloria promised to keep Ruth in the loop and then made her way out of the post office and over to Dot's.

She stepped inside, her eyes searching for her friends, who were off in the far corner, huddled around a table.

Gloria nodded at several restaurant patrons as she hobbled to the back. Margaret and Lucy were already there, along with Andrea and Eleanor.

Dot hovered off to one side as she shifted water glasses from her tray to the table. "Heard there's been another unfortunate death in town."

It had been a while since the town of Belhaven had been rocked by scandal, if you didn't count Cal Evergreen, the county commissioner, who had been charged with extortion just days before Christmas.

It had been quite some time since a death had shadowed their small town...until now.

Lucy pulled out an empty chair for Gloria and reached for her crutches. "When are you getting that crazy cast off?"

"Not soon enough," Gloria groaned and backed onto the chair. "Ruth and Judith Arnett just told me Carl saw Ed Mueller arguing with Officer Joe Nelson in front of the Quik Stop last night."

Eleanor gasped. "My goodness. I think..." her voice trailed off.

"Yes?" Gloria prompted.

Eleanor's face became blank. "I can't remember." Her hand trembled slightly as she reached for her water glass. "There's something stuck in the back of my head. I wish I could reach back there and pull it out."

Margaret patted her hand. "Happens to all of us Eleanor. It will probably come to you when you least expect it."

"I'll be right back." Dot darted to the kitchen. She returned a short time later with a platter of fresh-from-the-oven chocolate chip cookies and walnut brownies.

Ray, Dot's husband, trailed behind with a pot of coffee and stack of coffee mugs. "It's nice to see you out and about, Eleanor," Ray said as he poured a cup of coffee and set it in front of her.

"Gloria was kind enough to include me in the group." Eleanor smiled at Gloria, who felt about an inch tall. It was a shame she didn't have more time to spend with Eleanor and others like her, who had no means of getting around and depended on the kindness of others.

She vowed to not only continue the Sunday visits with Eleanor, but to also check in with her during the week to see if she needed anything or perhaps even offer to take her with her sometimes.

The girls munched on the goodies and discussed Ed Mueller's death. She wondered if Ed's wife, Sheryl, knew yet.

First, there was the death of Ed's sister and now Ed's untimely demise. Gloria hoped Ed had a will. Perhaps Ed had killed himself.

They would have to wait for the autopsy results to find out. Officer Joe Nelson had made it clear he wasn't going to discuss the preliminary investigation.

Mally, who had crawled under the table and taken a light nap, began to whine.

Gloria tilted her head and peeked under the table. "I better take Mally out for a break."

Andrea hopped up. "I'll take her," she offered.

"Thanks Andrea."

Gloria watched as Mally and Andrea made their way out the front door and past the large picture window. "They're probably going to visit Brian."

Brian was Brian Sellers. He owned Belhaven's hardware store, Nails and Knobs, the pharmacy and Quik Stop, the corner grocery.

Brian had recently proposed to Andrea and an engagement party was in the works.

Andrea was like a second daughter to Gloria and Brian, like a son. Gloria was tickled pink at the engagement announcement and a summer wedding was in the planning stages.

Andrea and Mally returned a short time later, followed by Ruth.

"I gotta make it quick. Kenny is covering for me." Ruth pulled a chair from the empty table beside them and dragged it to the table. "So what did I miss?"

Lucy and Margaret shifted their chairs to make room for Ruth to squeeze in.

"Not much." Lucy reached for a brownie. "Eleanor said she thinks there's something she's forgetting."

Dot slid out of her seat, ran to the back and returned with a cup of coffee for Ruth. She handed the steaming cup to her friend. "We've been trying to jog her memory but no luck so far."

"Thanks Dot." Margaret lifted the coffee cup and took a sip. "Don and I were in the Middle East one time and watched a man hypnotize another man to jog his memory." She shifted her gaze. "What do you think Eleanor?"

Eleanor shrank back in the chair. "I-I don't know..."

Gloria wasn't sure, either. "Hypnosis?"

Eleanor pressed her index finger against the bridge of her wire-rimmed glasses and pushed. "Let me think about it."

Margaret leaned forward in her chair. "I can do some research. I've always been fascinated by hypnosis!"

Andrea glanced at her watch. "Oh my gosh! I almost forgot about Alice. I have to go pick her up at the puppy place!"

Alice worked at At Your Service, a dog-training center, along with Mario Acosta, who owned the company.

They had just begun matching the first wave of trained dogs with new owners. Along with the training center, they ran a thriving boarding kennel.

Business was booming and Gloria, who had helped get the business up and running by loaning them money, was making a tidy return on her initial investment.

"I can drive out there to pick her up," Gloria offered. She glanced at Eleanor. "Is that okay Eleanor?"

Eleanor nodded. "Sure. You can take me home afterwards."

The women and Mally headed toward the front door and exited the restaurant. They crossed the street and climbed into Gloria's car.

The Acosta farm and At Your Service were several miles from town, out in the country, and Gloria was thankful the roads were clear.

When they got there, Gloria and Eleanor waited in the car while Andrea headed to the building that housed the At Your Service kennel.

Eleanor watched Andrea disappear inside the building. "What do you think of Margaret hypnotizing me?"

Gloria rubbed the side of her forehead. On the one hand, she was dying to know what it was Eleanor couldn't remember. On the other hand, Margaret was no "hypnosis expert."

Not only that, Gloria thought hypnosis was a bunch of baloney.

"It would have to be your decision," Gloria finally said. She wondered if Margaret would make Eleanor bark like a dog or some other silly command Gloria had seen hypnotists do.

Andrea returned with Alice in tow. The women climbed in the back seat and reached for their seatbelts.

Mally promptly sniffed Alice and then licked her arm. Alice wrapped her arms around Mally's neck and hugged her. "Hello Mally. I haven't seen you in ages." She patted Mally's back and she laid her head in Alice's lap.

"The dog whisperer," Gloria teased as she glanced in the rearview mirror.

"I'm surprise you all come to pick me up," Alice said in her thick Spanish accent. She turned to Eleanor. "You are Miss Gloria's friend?"

"Shame on me!" Gloria gasped. "Alice, this is Eleanor. Eleanor this is Alice."

"Nice to meet you," Eleanor said.

"Oh. It is nice to meet you, Miss Eleanor."

On the drive back, the girls filled Alice in on the day. When Alice found out a summer resident's body had been found in a shanty, she made a cross symbol across her chest. "I pray for his soul."

When they reached Andrea and Alice's place, the two women climbed out of the car. "Oh! Wait Miss Gloria. I have some ting *very* special to give you." She held up an index finger. "I be right back."

Alice sprinted around the side of the car and disappeared inside the house.

"What is she getting?" Gloria asked Andrea.

"Oh my goodness!" Andrea grinned and shook her head. "I'll let her explain it to you."

Alice returned a few moments later carrying a small paper sack. She made her way over to the driver's side window and held it out. "Take this home. It is a special spice...for lovers."

Gloria's face turned beet red as she reached for the package. "Th-thanks, Alice." Not sure what else to say, she opened the top and peeked inside at the small, plastic container. "What's in it?"

"Oh," Alice clasped her hands together. "You doan wanna know. If you in the mood for a little love, mix just a pinch in your food." She placed her thumb and forefinger close together, leaving only a small space in between. "Just a little. It go a loooong way."

Gloria turned her gaze to Andrea, who shrugged her shoulders. "I have no idea what she put in it, but I would heed her advice and not use too much."

Gloria thanked her a second time and then waited while Andrea and Alice headed inside. When Alice reached the door, she turned around and gave Gloria a thumb up.

"My," Eleanor glanced at the brown paper bag sitting on the seat between them. "I've never heard of such a thing."

"Me either," Gloria said. She pulled into Eleanor's drive and stopped the car near the front steps.

Eleanor reached for the door handle. "You don't have to get out," she told Gloria.

"Okay." Gloria nodded. "I'll wait until you get inside before I leave." She watched Eleanor climb out of the car, reach inside the back seat for her walker and then turn to close the door. "I'll call you if I remember."

Gloria nodded. "Thanks Eleanor. Be careful going up the steps."

Eleanor closed the rear passenger door and slowly made her way up the steps and inside the house. Gloria waited until Eleanor waved before pulling out of the drive and heading home.

Paul would be home soon, and Gloria hadn't given dinner a single thought. If it had been just her, she would've thrown leftovers or a frozen dinner in the microwave and called it good, but Paul and she were still newlyweds and still adjusting to living together.

She mentally ticked off the items in her fridge and by the time Gloria pulled the car in the garage, she had decided on hot ham and cheese sandwiches along with tomato soup. It was the perfect meal for a cold winter night.

The first thing Gloria did when she got inside the house was shove Alice's love potion in the far corner of the pantry. She wasn't quite sure what to think of it and decided she would try to dissect it when she had more time.

It was dusk when Paul arrived and Gloria met him at the door. "I missed you today," she said as he kissed her lips and pulled her into a warm embrace.

Paul reluctantly released his hold on his new bride, shrugged out of his winter jacket and hung it on the hook by the door. "I figured you'd be knee deep investigating the death of the man whose body was found out on Lake Terrace."

Gloria hobbled to the kitchen sink. "Well, I'm not knee deep in it yet. So you heard?"

Paul nodded. "Yeah. One of the other security guys, an off-duty cop, told me about it. Said the guy was found inside his ice shanty out on the lake."

Gloria's investigative antenna shot up, on high alert. "Have investigators determined a cause of death?"

"No. Only that the lower half of his body was frozen in the ice."

Chapter 4

Gloria shuddered. "What a terrible way to die, trapped in the ice and freezing to death."

"Investigators don't believe that he froze to death," Paul said.

"But how did he..." Gloria started to ask, but Paul was already shaking his head.

From the look on her husband's face, she knew she was wasting her breath.

Gloria gathered all of the sandwich ingredients and made her way over to the kitchen stove.

Paul had gotten creative and placed wooden benches in front of both the kitchen sink and stove so Gloria could rest her broken leg on the bench while she worked. "I heard Officer Joe Nelson was seen arguing with Ed Mueller last night."

Paul, a retired Montbay County Sheriff, had worked with the other officer on numerous occasions. The two men weren't friends, but were friendly with one another and Paul had nothing but respect for his former fellow officer.

"Who told you that?" Paul removed his wet work boots and placed them on the boot tray next to the porch door.

"Judith Arnett. Her husband, Carl, spotted them out in front of the Quik Stop."

She went on. "Eleanor Whittaker, the lady who lives on the hill overlooking Lake Terrace, called me this morning to tell me something was going on."

Paul shuffled to the kitchen sink. He turned the faucet on, squirted a glob of soap in his hands and scrubbed them under the running water. "So you decided to run right down there and find out what was going on?"

Gloria shrugged. "Sort of. Officer Joe Nelson and Officer Smith made all of us leave the area. I barely had enough time to scope out Mueller's cottage."

Paul ripped a paper towel from the paper towel holder and dried his hands. "You went inside the dead man's cottage?"

Gloria grabbed the spatula and flipped the ham and cheese sandwich to toast the other side. "Yeah. I only got a brief look around before Officer Joe Nelson told me I had to leave."

"Ed Mueller was in town last night but when I checked the wood stove inside the cottage, it was cold. If Ed had spent the night in his cottage, it was a mighty cold one."

The sandwiches were ready and the soup hot.

Gloria let Paul carry the food to the table. She had made an extra sandwich and while Paul set the table, Gloria tore the sandwich into bite size pieces, giving the larger chunks to Mally and some of the smaller pieces to Puddles, her cat.

She shuffled to the kitchen table and settled into the chair next to her husband. After arranging her soup and sandwich in front of her, she bowed her head to pray.

Paul grasped her hand. "Dear Lord. Thank you for the food that you've given us. We pray for protection for not only us, but also our loved ones. Please help my wife's leg heal and the cast come off quickly."

"Amen," Gloria echoed with enthusiasm as she lifted her head and gazed out the window. With mention of a coming snow/ice storm, the last thing Gloria wanted to do was try to navigate a snowstorm on crutches.

Taking a fall at her age could be deadly and visions of a broken hip or busted rib were scary thoughts. She picked up half of her sandwich and tore the end off. "Was today the last day for the security detail?"

'Security Detail,' also known as 'Personal Security Detail,' assignments were lucrative extra income for Paul and Gloria. Not only was the extra money nice, it kept Paul somewhat busy.

When Paul first tossed around the idea of retiring from the police force, he had decided on a full retirement, but the more he and Gloria discussed it, the more Paul realized he would be bored out of his mind hanging around the farms.

There was only so much fishing and hunting, along with honey-do projects to keep him busy. The part-time work broke up his week, and Gloria didn't feel guilty when she wanted to hang out with her friends or perhaps even start a new investigation.

He nodded as he picked up his spoon. "I have tomorrow off and then two days working for another political candidate who has scheduled rallies in Grand Rapids."

The boys, Gloria's grandsons, Ryan and Tyler, had called earlier, right after Gloria had gotten home. The school had an in-service day and the boys had asked if they could visit.

Gloria had seen them briefly, when she'd picked up Mally the day Paul and she had returned from their honeymoon. She still hadn't given them the souvenirs she'd purchased in Florida. "Ryan and Tyler asked if they could spend the day over here. There's no school tomorrow."

Paul nodded and sipped his ice water. "Sure. Did you tell them about the metal detectors?"

"No. I wanted to surprise them." She couldn't wait to see the looks on their faces when they got their gifts and knew they would be anxious to try them out, although she wasn't sure how much they could find in the mud and muck that was now her yard and garden.

"I'll call them after we finish eating." She popped the last bite of sandwich in her mouth and emptied her soup bowl.

Paul offered to wash the dishes and Gloria headed to the house phone to call her grandsons. Tyler, the older of the two, answered the phone. "So can we come, Grams? We're already bored."

"Give me the phone!" Gloria could hear Ryan, her younger grandson, in the background.

"I had it first," Tyler insisted. "What time can we get there?"

"How does nine sound? It will give me time to get up and get around," Gloria said.

"We'll be there at nine, Grams," Tyler said. The line disconnected, but not before Gloria heard Ryan one final time. "I wanted to talk to her!" he wailed.

Gloria smiled as she replaced the receiver. She turned to Paul, who was standing in front of the kitchen sink. "They will be here at nine."

"We better get a good night's sleep," Paul joked as he handed Gloria her crutches and they made their way into the living room.

***

Gloria cradled her cup of coffee as she stared out the window and waited for her grandsons' arrival. She had spent the previous night tossing and turning in bed, her thoughts ping ponging between her excitement at seeing Ryan and Tyler and thinking about the poor man, Ed Mueller.

Had he accidentally fallen through? It was possible. She made a mental note to check with the others who had been there when his body had been discovered. Then she remembered someone saying they had covered his body because it wasn't a pretty sight.

It had been so hectic she hadn't had the time to study the ice or the shanty. Her broken leg had slowed her down and Gloria lost precious time trying to make it to the body without falling.

She also wondered if Eleanor finally remembered whatever had been nagging in the back of her mind and vowed to call her later that evening, after the boys left.

Jill's car pulled into the drive and barely stopped when the rear passenger doors swung open. The boys darted across the soggy yard, racing each other to the porch.

Gloria set her coffee cup on the kitchen table, opened the door and stepped onto the porch. "We stayed awake all night 'cuz we couldn't sleep," Ryan told his grandmother when he got close.

She wrapped both arms around her youngest grandson. "That makes three of us." Gloria hugged Tyler next and then her daughter, Jill, who rolled her eyes. "They have been driving me nuts!"

Tyler cut his mother off. "What did you get us in Florida, Grams? Did you bring us back an alligator?" He turned to his brother. "That would be cool! We would be the only ones in our whole school to have a pet alligator."

Gloria quickly burst their bubble. "No, I did not bring back an alligator." She thought about Rumble and Thunder, the resident alligators Liz, Frances and she had encountered.

Ryan's smile faded, but he quickly brightened. "How 'bout a lizard. I heard they have lizards in Florida."

Gloria shook her head. "No, I didn't bring back a lizard, either. In fact, I didn't bring any living creature back."

Jill's hand flew to her chest. "Thank heavens!"

Gloria hobbled over to the corner of the kitchen, picked up the two store bags she'd gotten from the beach shop and handed one to Tyler and the other to Ryan.

Ryan and Tyler tore the tops of their bags open and reached inside. "Cool!" Ryan's eyes gleamed. "Can we try them out?"

The ground was wet but still frozen solid. She doubted the boys would be able to get a hit on anything in the yard. "Try the barn first," Gloria suggested.

The boys headed to the barn while Gloria walked her daughter, Jill, to her car. "What time would you like me to pick the boys up?"

Gloria would've loved for them to spend the night but they had school the next day and would have to save the sleepover for another time. "Paul and I plan to take them down to Dot's Restaurant for dinner so maybe around seven?"

"Sounds good." Jill nodded and then hugged her mother. "Thanks for saving my sanity," she joked.

Paul, who had been puttering around in the workshop he'd set up in the garage, came out to say hello. "Did your mom tell you about the summer resident whose body was found in his ice shanty?"

Jill, halfway in her car, paused. "Who was that?"

Many of the summer cottages had been family-owned for decades and passed down from generation to generation. During the summer months, the "city" kids would hang out with the local kids and many of them formed friendships that lasted a lifetime.

"Ed Mueller," Gloria said.

"The first cottage at the bottom of the hill, right on the lake?"

Gloria nodded. "Yeah. His body was found partially submerged in the ice."

Jill wrinkled her nose. "Ew. What a terrible way to die. Did he accidentally fall through and then couldn't pull himself back out?"

"Good question," Gloria said. *And one I intend to find the answer to* she added silently.

They watched Jill back out of the drive and pull onto the road.

Gloria slipped her arm through Paul's. "Perhaps I can accompany you to the workshop?" she asked.

"Nice try!" Paul said. He had spent his last several free days holed up in his workshop, working on a "secret" project. Every time Gloria tried to find out what kind of project he was working on, he clammed up.

She knew he loved woodworking projects and had handcrafted some lovely birdhouses, along with a magazine rack Gloria had placed next to her recliner. She couldn't wait to find out what he was making and the suspense was killing her!

Patience wasn't Gloria's strong suit, but she was trying. To ensure her curiosity didn't get the better of her, Paul had placed a padlock on the workshop door.

"Grams! Come quick!" Ryan stood just inside the barn, waving his arms frantically in the air.

Chapter 5

Visions of Tyler hanging from the rafters again, or the boys having cornered some wild creature filled Gloria's head as she limped to the barn as quickly as possible, cursing the crutches every step of the way.

By the time Paul and she reached the barn doors, Ryan had disappeared.

"Ryan?"

"In here." Tyler's voice rang out from the direction of the milking parlor.

Paul led the way and Gloria followed behind as they made their way across the cement barn floor and to the milking parlor.

The boys, metal detectors in hand, stood peering down into the center floor drain. A portion of the grate consisted of thick wood and the outer edge was metal.

Ryan pointed. "There's something down there."

Gloria shuffled forward. "Where? Are you sure the metal detectors aren't going off because of the metal?"

"Nope. There's something in there. See those shiny things?"

She tipped her head to the side and caught a glimpse of several small, round objects. "We need a flashlight."

"I'll get it!" Tyler raced out of the barn and headed to the garage where he knew his grandmother kept a heavy-duty flashlight.

He returned moments later and handed it to Paul, who turned it on and aimed the light toward the grate. "Yeah. There's something down in there."

He lowered onto one knee and grasped the sides of the grate. Using both hands, he gave it a firm tug. It wouldn't budge. "The grate is screwed into the cement floor."

Gloria wasn't sure how long the grate had been in place but it had been there for many years, so many she had no idea when the grate had been installed.

"I'll go get the drill." Paul stood, brushed the dirt from his pant leg and walked out of the milking parlor.

Ryan and Tyler dropped down onto their hands and knees and peered into the grate.

Tyler stuck his fingers between the slats. "I can touch something."

Ryan, not to be out done by his older brother, stuck his hand in another slat. "Me too."

When Paul returned, he removed the drill from the case, placed a drill bit in the drill and knelt down next to the corner plate.

He placed the bit in the slots of the screw and pressed the *on* switch.

Burrupp!

Paul turned the drill off. "The screw is stripped." He moved to the other corner and tried again.

Buzz.

Burrupp!

He shut the drill off and leaned back. "This isn't going to work. The screws are stripped." He set the drill on the cement floor. "We're gonna have to try to pry it off."

Gloria wasn't concerned about damaging the decades-old barn floor. The milking parlor hadn't been used in years. "As long as we can place the grate back on top so no one falls into the drain, then pry away."

Paul headed out of the barn a second time to search for a crowbar and hammer.

Ryan and Tyler crawled forward and Ryan stuck his fingers inside the slats again. "I can try to move them to the end." He wiggled his fingers.

"Ouch!" Ryan tugged on his hand. "My hand! It's stuck!"

Gloria shifted on her crutches. "Ryan Adams. That's not funny!"

Ryan's lower lip started to quiver. "I'm not kidding, Grams. My fingers are stuck," he yelped.

Gloria inched closer and bent forward, balancing on her one good foot. She could see his fingers were indeed stuck between two slats. "Oh good heavens! Don't pull. It will only make it worse," she warned and then turned to Tyler. "Go get the bottle of vegetable oil in the kitchen pantry."

Tyler jumped to his feet and darted to the door. "Bring some Q-tips from the bathroom, too," she hollered after him.

Tyler passed Paul, who was on his way back with a hammer and crowbar. "Where's he going?" Paul asked as he stepped into the milking parlor.

"Ryan's fingers are stuck in the grates. I sent him into the house to get some vegetable oil and Q-tips."

Paul set the tools on the floor, and knelt next to Ryan, whose eyes were full of unshed tears. "Hang in there, buddy. Your fingers will be free in a jiffy," he said as he patted his back.

"Here you go, Grams!" Tyler had returned with the vegetable oil and Q-tips in hand.

"Set them next to Ryan." Gloria turned to Paul. "Help me get down on the floor."

Paul wrapped his arm around Gloria's waist and slowly lowered her onto the milking parlor floor.

She scooched forward so she was within easy reach of her grandson. "Close your eyes," she told him.

Ryan obediently shut his eyes while Gloria removed the cap on the vegetable oil and poured a generous amount onto several of the Q-tips.

Next, she doused her young grandson's hand with the oil and then slipped her index finger next to his. She wiggled gently.

The two fingers that were stuck shifted apart. With space in between, she rubbed the Q-tip coated with oil between his fingers. "Try moving them," she said.

Ryan sucked in a breath and pulled. His fingers popped out of the grate.

He held his fingers up for a closer inspection. "I think they're broken," he sniffed.

Gloria gently lifted his hand and studied the angry red slash that marked the spot where the fingers had been stuck. She gently bent both fingers. "No. They just got pinched."

Tyler placed a hand on his hip and gazed down at his younger brother. "You shouldn't have stuck your fingers so far down."

"You did the same thing," Ryan insisted.

"Boys!" Gloria refereed. "Let's see if we can get this grate off."

The boys, their argument quickly forgotten, leaned close as Paul made his way to the corner. He placed the flat end of the crowbar under the edge of the grate and leveraged his weight against the long end.

The grate wouldn't budge.

Paul reached for the hammer. He began to tap on the end of the crowbar. "It's starting to give."

Gloria, still sitting on the floor, inched forward.

Paul removed the crowbar and shifted to the other side. "We better loosen this corner, too."

Once again, he placed the flat end of the crowbar under the edge of the grate and tapped on the long end with the hammer.

The grate visibly shifted.

"I think we're making some progress." Paul shifted back to the other side and repeated the process until the ends broke free.

He carefully lifted the grate and set it off to the side.

They all leaned forward and gazed into the drain. Inside the drain were several coins, along with a metal object.

Gloria plucked the metal object from the drain and rolled it over in the palm of her hand. It was a button. "Well, I'll be. It says 'Rutherford and Sons,'" she whispered.

Sudden tears burned the back of Gloria's eyes. The button was from a pair of farm overalls that not only had her first husband, James, worn, but also James's father and grandfather. It had been years since she'd seen one of the buttons, let alone the overalls.

Gloria tucked the tiny treasure in her pants pocket and blinked back sudden tears.

The boys had already gathered up the coins and began inspecting them. "These are just some dirty old pennies," Tyler scoffed.

"Don't be so sure," Gloria warned. "We should take them inside and clean them up."

Tyler and Ryan handed the dirty coins to Gloria, who dropped them in her pocket next to the treasured button.

Tyler reached inside his jacket pocket and pulled out a round, tarnished metal object. "We found this over in the corner."

Chapter 6

They all turned their attention to the metal trinket. It reminded Gloria of a vase. She reached out and took the object from Tyler, holding it up for closer examination.

A thick layer of gray dirt coated the exterior. Gloria ran her finger around the outer rim and then blew on the top.

"It looks like an old spittoon," Paul remarked.

Gloria wrinkled her nose as she twisted it between her fingers. "You're right. Now that I think about it, James's father chewed tobacco."

"What's a spuddune?" Tyler asked.

"It's a spittoon," Gloria corrected. "Years ago, instead of smoking tobacco – or cigarettes – it was popular to chew tobacco. People used these spittoons to spit the chewed tobacco in."

Ryan wrinkled his brows and stared at the spittoon. "Gross. That's disgusting!"

Paul took the spittoon from Gloria. "Back in the day, folks didn't know how dangerous it was to chew or smoke tobacco."

"My grandmother and grandfather used to chew tobacco," Gloria told her grandsons.

Tyler's eyes widened in horror. "You didn't chew tobacco, did you Grams?"

Gloria grinned and shook her head. "No, Tyler. I did not."

The boys finished inspecting the drain. When they were certain there were no more "treasures" to be found, Paul replaced the grate and hammered the corners down.

After ensuring the grate was in place, he stood and brushed off the front of his slacks. "Any more hits on the metal detectors?"

Tyler's shoulders slumped. "No. We checked the whole barn."

Ryan lightly tapped the tip of the metal detector on the cement floor. "Uh-uh. What about Mally? She was beeping."

Mally, who had been sniffing the perimeter of the barn's interior, heard her name and trotted over.

Ryan switched his metal detector on and ran the wand over Mally. The detector began beeping and increased in beeps as Ryan placed the end against her abdomen.

Gloria frowned and then turned to Paul. "You don't think she ate the key ring?"

Paul had placed a leather key ring on the corner cabinet near the kitchen table earlier that morning. Fortunately, there were no keys on the ring, but the leather ring was missing.

"Mally, did you swallow the key ring?" Gloria shifted on her crutches.

Mally whined and thumped her tail.

Gloria reached down and patted her head. "We better go inside and call the vet to see what he thinks."

Paul waited for Ryan, Tyler, Gloria and Mally to step out of the barn before pulling the barn doors closed and placing the padlock on the door.

Paul headed to the workshop and Gloria and the boys headed to the house. When they got inside the kitchen, Gloria made a beeline for the home phone. Ken Bailey, Mally's vet, was on Gloria's speed dial.

The call went directly to voice mail. Gloria briefly explained the situation and asked the vet to call her back as soon as possible.

"We're hungry," Ryan announced, when they reached the house.

Gloria had thawed two plastic baggies filled with pulled pork barbeque she'd made in her crockpot a few days earlier.

She put Ryan and Tyler in charge of setting the table while she kept one eye on Mally, looking for signs that she had eaten something she wasn't supposed to.

Mally, meanwhile, kept a close eye on the boys, hoping one of them would give her a treat.

Gloria made her way over to the freezer, opened the door and peered inside. She grabbed an unopened bag of tater tots. Balancing the tater tots bag in one hand, she hobbled across the room.

She turned the oven on, dumped the tater tots on a cookie sheet and spread them out.

The kitchen phone began ringing.

Tyler reached for the phone. "You want me to answer the phone Grams?"

Gloria nodded. "It's probably Dr. Bailey."

"Hello? Just a second." Tyler covered the mouthpiece with his hand. "Yep. It's Dr. Bailey." He walked over to his grandmother and handed her the phone.

"Hello Doctor Bailey. Thank you for calling me back." Gloria briefly explained for a second time her concern that Mally had swallowed not only the leather part of the key chain but also the metal ring.

She told the vet how the boys had gotten a *ping* from a metal detector when they placed it near her stomach.

Dr. Bailey spoke. "Is she acting unusual? Does she seem to be in pain?"

Gloria gazed at her beloved pooch, who was standing next to Ryan with her mouth open, begging for a treat. "No. She acts peppy. Her appetite seems good."

"You can bring her in for an x-ray if you're concerned. We're open until five."

"I-I think I will. We will be there around one." She could take the boys with her. She hung up the phone and turned her attention to the task at hand, anxious to finish lunch and get to the vet.

Paul stepped into the kitchen just as she was getting ready to call him inside for lunch.

"Your timing is impeccable," Gloria remarked. "I talked to the vet and told him I would feel better if he took an x-ray of Mally, just to make sure she hadn't swallowed the key ring."

Paul hung his jacket on the hook near the door, plopped down in the chair and pulled his boots off. "Do you want me to go with you?"

Paul had committed to security detail for the rest of the week. Today was his only day off. "The boys can go with me," she said.

Paul made his way to the kitchen sink, washed his hands and reached for a paper towel. "I don't mind."

Ryan pulled out a kitchen chair and sat down. "We can go with Grams."

Paul gazed at Ryan thoughtfully. "I'll let you three go, then," he said. "As long as you're sure."

"I'm sure," Gloria said.

They settled into the chairs around the table and Paul eyed the large bowl of pulled pork. "Looks delicious," he said before they all bowed their heads to pray.

Paul prayed over the food and Gloria added the ending. "Please watch over Mally until we can get to the vet."

"Amen!"

Gloria reached inside the bread bag, grabbed a hamburger bun and passed the package to Ryan, who took two buns and handed the package to his brother.

It was a good thing she'd thawed two packages of leftover pulled pork. She had forgotten how much the boys could eat!

Gloria kept her attention focused on Mally the entire time she ate. When she finished eating, she wiped her mouth with her napkin and placed it on top of her empty plate.

Paul, noting her concerned expression, reached over and squeezed her hand. "You go on ahead to the vet. I'll stay here and clean up."

"You're sure?" she asked.

"Yep. I'm positive." Paul nodded.

"Okay. Thanks." She made a quick trip to the bathroom. The boys and Mally were waiting by the door when she returned.

Paul had pulled the car out of the garage and parked it next to the steps.

Gloria gave her husband a quick kiss. "Thanks. We'll be back as soon as possible."

Although the veterinarian was in Green Springs, which was only about a twenty-minute drive from the farm, the trip seemed to take forever.

Forecasters had predicted the winter storm would start early the next morning and Gloria was relieved the roads were still clear.

The vet's parking lot was nearly empty and when they got inside, there was only one person seated in the lobby.

Gloria hobbled to the desk. "Hi. I'm Gloria Ru-Kennedy. I spoke with Dr. Bailey a short time ago on the phone. He said I could bring my dog, Mally, in for an emergency visit. We think she may have swallowed something."

The dark-haired woman nodded. "He's in the middle of an exam but shouldn't be long."

Gloria settled into the chair closest to the front. Mally flopped down on top of Gloria's feet and she leaned over to study her pooch.

Mally didn't appear to be in pain but Gloria knew she wouldn't be able to rest or focus on anything else until she was certain Mally wasn't in any danger.

"Mally?"

Dr. Bailey appeared from around the corner. Mally scrambled to her feet and began wagging her tail as she trotted to him.

When she got close to the vet, he reached down and patted her head. "Don't you know that the only thing you're supposed to eat is dog food?"

Gloria glanced at her grandsons. "You stay here."

Mally and Gloria followed the vet down the hall and into an examination room.

"What did you do to your leg, young lady?" The doctor asked Gloria as they made their way into the room.

Gloria rolled her eyes. "It's a long story."

"Another investigation?" he teased. Gloria had met Dr. Bailey some time ago, after her friend, Margaret, and she had taken a trip to the Smoky Mountains to chase after Gloria's sister, Liz.

During the trip, which included a visit to their long lost relative, Aunt Ethel, Mally had been shot and Gloria had taken her to an area hospital emergency room for treatment.

When she returned to Belhaven, Mally and she visited Dr. Bailey so he could check on her wound.

"You could say that," Gloria admitted.

The doctor set the clipboard he was holding on the counter nearby, rested both hands on top of his legs and bent down to Mally's level. "Well? What have you got to say about all of this?"

Mally licked the side of his face. He laughed and patted the top of the examining table. "Hop up here so we can take a picture of you," he told the dog.

Gloria's beloved pooch tilted her head and stared at the vet but didn't budge. Dr. Bailey reached inside his lab coat and pulled out a doggie treat. He held the treat so that it dangled over the top of the examining table.

That was all the persuasion needed as Mally promptly jumped up on the examining table and took the treat from the vet's hand.

Dr. Bailey turned to Gloria as he reached for a lead apron hanging on a hook nearby and slipped it over his head.

"I'm going to take the x-ray now. Wait just outside and I'll let you know when I'm done."

Gloria nodded and then hobbled into the hall.

The vet closed the door behind her.

Gloria leaned her back against the hall wall, closed her eyes and prayed. "Please God. Protect Mally."

The door popped open and Dr. Bailey stuck his head around the corner. "You can come back in now."

Gloria limped into the room, her gaze shifting to her beloved dog, who looked quite comfortable lying on the table. She lifted her head and thumped her tail when she saw Gloria.

"I'll be back shortly with the x-rays," the doctor said as he exited the room.

Gloria paced, or more like limped, back and forth across the small examination room, anxious for the results.

The doctor stepped back into the room a short time later holding a set of x-rays. "I have some good news and some bad news."

Chapter 7

Dr. Bailey held one of the x-rays up to the ceiling light and pointed at the center. "See the small, round object?"

"Yes."

"Is that the size of the key ring?"

Gloria narrowed her eyes and studied the object. "Yes. Yes, I think it is."

Dr. Bailey held the second x-ray to the light. "This is a different angle but you can see the round object there."

Gloria nodded. "Now what?"

"The good news is the ring is still inside her stomach. Mally hasn't started trying to digest it...yet. The bad news is that it has to come out."

Gloria's heart began to thump loudly and her stomach churned. "H-how?"

Dr. Bailey set the x-rays on the counter, grabbed a notepad and pen near the back of the counter and began scribbling on the notepad. "This is the cheapest and fastest way to get rid of the ring. It works like a charm...99.9% of the time."

"Will we have to wait for her to pass it?"

He shook his head. "Nope. She's going to have to throw it up."

Gloria pulled on the bottom of her sweater and gazed at her dog.

Dr. Bailey continued to scribble on the piece of paper. When he finished, he ripped the sheet from the pad and handed it to Gloria. "Mix these ingredients together but don't add the hydrogen peroxide until the very end."

He went on. "This should work but if it doesn't, call me."

"If it doesn't work..." Gloria's voice trailed off.

"Then we'll have to surgically remove the ring."

Gloria glanced at the paper, folded it in half and tucked it in her purse.

"Like I said, it works almost all the time," Dr. Bailey said. "Just make sure you're outside because when she throws up, there won't be any warning."

Dr. Bailey signaled for Mally to hop off the examining table. "C'mon girl. Time to go home."

Mally and Gloria followed Dr. Bailey to the waiting room. "If she won't eat the squash, flax seed and meat, a simpler recipe is one teaspoon of hydrogen peroxide for every ten pounds Mally weighs. Mix it with a little vanilla ice cream." He set Mally's chart on the counter. "Either way, give me a call." He reached down and patted Mally's head.

"Will do." Gloria placed her purse on the counter and waited while the receptionist finished the paperwork.

"Today's office visit will be fifty dollars," the woman said.

Gloria reached inside her purse, pulled out her wallet and handed the woman her debit card.

The woman scanned the card and then handed it and a receipt to Gloria.

"What did he say Grams?" Ryan came up beside Gloria and tugged on her elbow.

"The vet found a ring in Mally's tummy. We have to make her a special concoction to eat so that she'll throw it up."

Gloria glanced at her beloved pooch. Poor Mally. She didn't look like she was in pain... Of course, she wasn't trying to digest the ring - yet.

When they reached the car, the boys and Mally hopped in the back seat.

Gloria started the car and glanced in the rearview mirror. "We'll have to stop at the grocery store to pick up a couple things."

She decided to purchase the items on the list at the large supermarket in Green Springs. The Quik Stop in Belhaven might not have what she needed.

Gloria pulled the car into an empty parking spot, shifted into park and shut the engine off. She pulled the doctor's handwritten recipe from her purse. "Squash, flax seed, a small amount of liver or fish and hydrogen peroxide. As a backup plan, we'll get some vanilla ice cream."

"I hope they have flax seed," Gloria muttered as she reached for the door handle. "Mally, you'll have to stay here."

The boys climbed out of the backseat and the three of them made their way inside. Luckily, Gloria was able to find a small packet of flax seed. She grabbed the other ingredients, and then they stopped in the frozen food section for a quart of vanilla ice cream.

Tyler watched as his grandmother set the ice cream in the shopping cart. "Can we get some chocolate syrup to squirt on top?"

"And M&M's?" Ryan asked.

Gloria let the boys each pick out one topping for the ice cream before they headed to the checkout lane.

After the clerk bagged the groceries, Ryan picked up the bag with the squash and flax seed while Tyler grabbed the ice cream and toppings.

Ryan switched the grocery bag from one hand to the other. "Is Mally going to eat the yucky stuff?"

"Unfortunately, yes, at least I hope so." Gloria sighed. "Then she's going to throw it up. If that doesn't work, we'll mix the bubbly stuff with a little ice cream."

"Ew," Ryan gasped. "I would probably try it mixed with ice cream."

When they reached the farm, Paul was nowhere in sight but the kitchen was spotless.

Tyler dropped the bag of groceries on the kitchen counter. "When can we make the stuff that's gonna make Mally barf?"

"In a minute," Gloria said. *The sooner the better* she added silently.

Gloria placed her purse on the kitchen chair.

Chirp.

Her cell phone began to ring. She slipped her reading glasses on and gazed at the screen. It was Eleanor Whittaker.

"Hello?" She motioned for the boys to put the ice cream in the freezer and then turned her attention to Eleanor.

"Hi Gloria." Eleanor's small voice replied. Gloria turned the volume all the way up so she could hear Eleanor speak.

"I hope I'm not bothering you," Eleanor apologized.

"No bother, Eleanor. I have a small crisis with Mally but I have a minute to talk."

She waved at Ryan and Tyler to put the recipe items on the kitchen counter and to get a small mixing bowl from the cupboard. "Is everything alright?"

"Yes. I-I just wanted to say I remembered a vehicle pulling into the Mueller's drive the other night. It was dusk."

"Do you remember what kind of car?" That could be a huge clue!

"No. I've tried and tried and it's driving me nuts. I've been thinking...I would be willing to let Margaret try to hypnotize me."

Gloria squeezed her eyes shut. Margaret was not a professional hypnotist. What if she messed up and scarred poor Eleanor for life? She vowed to do a little research before calling Margaret and giving her the "good news."

"I'll check with Margaret and call you back," Gloria promised.

She hung up the phone and turned her attention to the array of items on her kitchen counter. "First, we have to take care of Mally."

Gloria cooked the squash in the microwave and at the same time boiled some water to mix with the flax seed.

After pureeing the squash, she mixed the squash with the flax seed and hot water and then added a small amount of smoked fish she had found in the deep freeze.

"Grab a paper plate," she told Tyler and then turned to Ryan. "Run into the bathroom and get the hydrogen peroxide. It's under the bathroom sink."

The boys brought the plate and peroxide to Gloria. She added the hydrogen peroxide, quickly placed the entire mixture on the plate and set it on the floor.

"C'mon Mally. Here's a treat," she coaxed.

Mally trotted to the plate, sniffed the mixture and promptly backed away.

"She doesn't like it Grams," Ryan said.

"We need to add a little something else to entice her," Gloria said. "How 'bout a little canned chicken from the fridge?"

Tyler raced to the fridge, yanked the door open and reached inside. He quickly returned with the plastic container.

Gloria scooped a large spoonful of chopped chicken and then pressed it into the center of the pile of bubbling mush.

Mally tiptoed over and sniffed the top. Deeming it now edible, she quickly devoured the plate of food.

Gloria clapped her hands. "Yes! Success!"

Ryan and Tyler did a high-five.

She reached down and picked up the empty paper plate. "Now it's time to head outside and wait."

The boys raced out the kitchen door and onto the porch. Mally was right behind them.

Tyler and Ryan darted around the yard, racing back and forth with Mally in hot pursuit.

Gloria glanced at her watch. Dr. Bailey had jotted a side note stating the mixture should work its magic in thirty minutes or less.

She settled onto the porch chair to wait, her eyes trained on her beloved pet.

The boys and Mally had stopped near the corner of the garden. Mally began heaving and the boys leaned over the top of her.

Tyler looked up. "Mally is barfing, Grams!"

Sure enough, Gloria's dog was heaving. "Thank you, God," Gloria whispered and then smiled. She never thought she would be thankful that her dog was throwing up. "Can you see anything?"

Ryan frowned and waved a hand across his face. "Nope. It's just a lot of stinky orangey stuff," he reported.

"Wait! I see something!" Tyler pointed.

Gloria eased out of the chair and made her way to the edge of the porch. "Does it look like a key ring?"

Tyler darted across the yard and over to a yellow birch tree near the edge of the garden. He picked up a fallen tree branch, raced back to Mally and Ryan, and began poking in the pile of puke. "Yeah."

Tyler lifted the branch. He was still too far away for Gloria to see so she stepped off the porch, crutches in tow. "Does it look like a key ring?"

Tyler and Ryan nodded in unison.

Tyler took a step toward his grandmother. "You want me to go rinse it off?"

Paul, hearing the commotion, appeared in the doorway of the garage. "You're back. Any luck at the vet?"

Tyler spun around. "Yeah. Mally just puked and this was inside the puke."

He shifted the stick so Paul could see. "Looks like the key ring in question," he said. "Let me grab the shovel and get rid of the pile." He disappeared inside the garage and returned moments later, shovel in hand.

Mally, who was now feeling much better, trotted over to Tyler and began sniffing the end of the stick.

"Oh no you don't!" Tyler swung the stick in the air and out of reach.

While Paul shoveled the pile of squash and carried it to the edge of the garden, Gloria made her way inside to grab a plastic grocery sack.

She stepped back onto the porch and held it up. "Ryan, give this to your brother so he can put the key ring inside and we can throw it away in the trash." She didn't want to chance Mally finding the key ring again and cause a re-enactment of the days' events.

Ryan grabbed the bag and darted over to his brother who was standing near the edge of the sidewalk.

Tyler waved the stick close to his brother's face. "I dare you to touch it," he taunted.

Ryan hopped backward. "Gross."

"Tyler," Gloria warned.

"O-kay!"

Ryan held the bag open and at a distance, while Tyler tilted the stick and the key ring dropped into the bottom of the open bag.

Ryan quickly tied the top shut and handed it to Paul, who had just returned from doggie duty.

Tyler ran to the edge of the garden, flung his arm back and then threw the stick into the field.

Mission accomplished, the boys darted across the lawn and came to an abrupt halt at the bottom of the steps. "That was fun!" Tyler said excitedly.

"Can we have some ice cream now?" Ryan asked.

Gloria held the kitchen door open and waited while Mally, Ryan and Tyler sprinted inside. "Yes! You both earned a big bowl of ice cream."

She waited for the boys to fix the bowls of ice cream before she limped to the dining room and settled into the chair in front of the computer.

It was time to do a little research on hypnosis.

Chapter 8

Gloria started to check her emails and then remembered she had promised to call Dr. Bailey to update him on the outcome of Mally's situation. She shifted in her chair. "Can one of you bring me the house phone?" she called out to the kitchen.

Ryan appeared moments later, phone in hand. "Thank you Ryan."

She turned the phone over and dialed the veterinarian's number. Dr. Bailey was with a four-legged patient, so Gloria left a message with the receptionist telling her Mally had "returned" the key ring and was feeling fine.

"Can we give Mally a taste of ice cream?" Mally patiently sat in front of the kitchen table and eyed the boys' treats.

"Just one large spoonful, but make sure it's just the vanilla ice cream with no chocolate or candies in it."

The boys proceeded to fight over who was going to give Mally the spoonful of ice cream. "You can both give Mally one spoonful," she said.

The compromise seemed to settle the argument and after Mally gobbled her treat, she trotted into the dining room and flopped down under the desk.

Gloria tilted her head and peered at her dog. "Those boys sure know how to wear you out, huh?"

Mally sighed and closed her eyes.

Tyler appeared in the doorway a short time later. "We rinsed our dishes and put them in the dishwasher. Can we go back outside?"

Ryan stood next to his brother. "Yeah. We still haven't gone into the front yard with the metal detectors."

"Yes, but stay away from the road," she said.

"Let's take them into the tree fort," Tyler told his brother as they slipped on their winter jackets and headed outdoors.

Mally, not wanting to miss the action, sprang to her feet and followed them outdoors.

Gloria turned in her chair and watched as they darted past the front window before turning her attention back to her search. She typed in "Process of Hypnosis" and clicked the enter key.

The first item to pop up was a video on hypnosis.

She clicked the video, turned the volume up and leaned forward. A flickering candle appeared and a man began speaking in a low voice, so low that Gloria had to turn the volume to the highest level to hear.

"Relax your body, relax your thoughts..." The man's voice droned on for several minutes and Gloria's mind began to drift, not to a state of relaxation, but to mull over poor Ed Mueller's demise. What was the reason for Mueller and Officer Joe Nelson's argument in front of the Quik Stop?

Had Eleanor caught a glimpse of Mueller's truck parked in the cottage drive?

Gloria shut off the video, still unsure if hypnosis was something they should mess with.

Gloria's home phone began ringing. "Hello?"

"It's me. Margaret. Eleanor called to say she wants to try the hypnosis thingy."

"I don't know..." Gloria's voice trailed off.

Margaret interrupted. "Well, you don't have to come, but I'm going to Eleanor's tomorrow around ten to try it. I have a video and everything."

Gloria closed her eyes and took a deep breath. "I'll be there." Paul and Gloria planned to take the boys to Dot's for dinner. Hopefully she would have a chance to let the others know Margaret's plan for the next day.

Someone needed to supervise and that someone was going to be Gloria!

***

Gloria hopped to the front porch to check on her grandsons. She opened the screen door and peered out. She could hear the echo of their voices and the sound was coming from their tree fort.

She stepped out onto the top porch step and peered from side to side. "Where's Mally?" she hollered.

"In here." Ryan's head popped out of the front window of the tree fort. Mally's furry face appeared next to his.

"How did…" She was going to ask how in the world the boys managed to get Mally up into the tree fort but had second thoughts. Maybe she didn't want to know. "Be careful coming back down." She shut the door, shaking her head as she hobbled back to the dining room.

She folded the load of laundry she'd tossed into the dryer earlier in the day, and then carefully placed the folded laundry in the backpack Paul had brought home right after they returned from their honeymoon.

She slipped her arms through the shoulders straps and reached for her crutches. The backpack had been a lifesaver for Gloria.

She glanced through the front porch window as she headed through the dining room, into the living room and finally, the master bedroom.

Paul had also placed a small folding tray in the closet so she could set clothes and other items on top. "A couple more weeks," she muttered under her breath as she shrugged off the backpack.

She placed the backpack on the small table and unzipped the front. It was sometimes tricky balancing, but she had to admit it was getting a little easier.

After she finished hanging the last sweater on the hanger and placing it on the closet rod, she slung the empty backpack over her shoulders and headed back to the kitchen.

Gloria's stomach grumbled. She hadn't eaten a bowl of ice cream with the boys and lunch seemed like eons ago. She grabbed a bag of potato chips from the pantry and hopped to the kitchen table, sliding into the chair on the far wall, close to her corner cabinet.

She pulled her worn Bible from the shelf and flipped it open to the marker. Next, she slipped her reading glasses on, and popped a potato chip in her mouth.

"In him we were also chosen, having been predestined according to the plan of him who works out everything in conformity with the purpose of his will..." Ephesians 1:11 NIV

Gloria pulled her glasses from her face and gazed out the kitchen window as she contemplated the verse. The idea that God had destined her life from before she was ever even a twinkle in her father's eye was mind-boggling.

Not only had God planned every moment of her life, He knew that someday she would marry James and then Paul, she would have three wonderful children, and grandchildren and friends she dearly loved.

God also knew the moment she would take her last breath and leave this world for her eternal home.

Gloria read a few more minutes, tucked her marker between the pages and closed her Bible. She glanced at the clock. It was time for the boys..."her" boys to come in and get cleaned up for dinner.

She slipped into her jacket, grabbed her crutches and headed outside.

First, she stopped by the garage workshop. She could hear the whir of a table saw from behind the closed door. Gloria lightly tapped on the door.

The whir continued.

She tried knocking again, this time harder.

The noise stopped. Paul peeked out through a crack in the door and the smell of sawdust drifted out.

"It's time to get cleaned up. We're going to Dot's for dinner," she reminded him.

"I almost forgot. I'll be done in a minute."

Gloria nodded and headed out of the garage. She crossed over the sidewalk and limped to the front yard.

A brisk winter breeze whipped 'round the corner of the house. The cold air rushed up her shirtsleeves, chilling her to the bone.

She stopped under the tree, balancing on her crutches. "Hey boys! Time to come down and get cleaned up for dinner!"

Tyler's head appeared in the window. "What's for dinner?"

"We're going to Dot's Restaurant."

Tyler nodded and disappeared inside the tree fort. He re-emerged moments later through the fort door. Ryan was right behind him and Mally brought up the rear.

Gloria shifted her gaze from the fort to the ground. "How are you going to get Mally down?"

"Watch this!" Tyler held up an old brown potato sack. "We found this out in the barn."

"C'mon Mally." With a great deal of coaxing on Ryan's part, he was finally able to convince Mally to crawl inside.

Gloria could see her shift inside the bag and moments later, her furry face appeared.

"Ryan, you hold the other end."

Tied to each side of the sack was a long piece of twined rope. Tyler held onto one rope and Ryan held the other side.

The boys carefully lifted the bag, gently placed it over the side of the fort's porch and slowly lowered the bag to the ground.

When the bag reached the ground, Mally popped out of the bag and trotted over to Gloria, who patted her head. "That looked like loads of fun," she told her pooch.

Tyler backed down the tree fort steps, which were nailed to the side of the tree.

Ryan followed behind his older brother. "Uh-oh. We forgot the metal detectors."

Tyler scampered back up the tree, disappeared inside and returned moments later with the detectors in hand. He lowered the detectors to his brother and then descended once again. "I'm starving."

"Me too," Ryan said.

"Go inside and wash up. We'll be leaving shortly."

The boys raced ahead. Gloria and Mally brought up the rear. When they got to the porch, Paul was waiting by the door. "This afternoon flew by," he said as he held the door.

It had been quite an afternoon between Ryan getting his fingers stuck in the grate, a visit to the vet, finding out Mally had swallowed a key ring and then trying to get the key ring back. "No kidding," Gloria groaned.

After they finished cleaning up, the four of them hopped into the car. "I'm gonna eat five chili dogs," Ryan predicted.

Gloria adjusted her seatbelt and stared out the window. "Dot has a new dinner special and tonight it's all-you-can-eat goulash and French bread." Dot had been working on her new super-secret recipe and Gloria could hardly wait to try it.

It was only five o'clock when they pulled into an empty parking spot out front. The dinner crowd hadn't descended on Dot's yet and they had their pick of tables.

Gloria led the way, deciding on a table near the back.

Ray, who was standing in front of the pass-thru window that connected the kitchen with the server station, waved. He appeared moments later and approached the table with a tray full of glasses of ice water. "Dot mentioned you were stopping by for dinner."

He ruffled Ryan's hair. "I didn't know you were bringing the big eaters with you," he joked.

"We haven't eaten all day and I'm starving," Ryan grumbled.

"You have too." Gloria shook her head. "We had pulled pork sandwiches and tater tots for lunch."

"I'll bring you a quick snack," Ray promised. He turned to Gloria. "Dot had to run down to the Quik Stop. We ran out of butter, believe it or not."

He disappeared in the back and reappeared moments later with a tray of chips and large bowl of salsa.

"Well, there you are!" Gloria turned to see Dot hustling over to the table. "I didn't know you were bringing the boys."

"They're just here for the day," Gloria said.

Tyler reached for a tortilla chip. "Mally threw up."

Dot lifted a brow. "Oh no! I hope she's okay."

"Grams made her throw up," Ryan added.

Dot shifted the grocery sack and grinned. "You don't say."

Gloria rolled her eyes and reached for her water glass. "It's a long story," she mumbled.

"I'm sure it is." Dot patted her friend's arm. "Let me drop this off in the back. Do you know what you want to eat?"

"Three chili dogs, pizza, French fries and a chocolate shake," Ryan rattled off.

Tyler dipped his chip in the salsa and shoved the entire piece in his mouth. "I'll have the thame."

"Let's start with two chili dogs each and two orders of fries," Gloria said. "I'll take an order of the goulash." She rubbed her hands together. "I've been dying to try it."

Paul leaned back in his chair. "I'll have the goulash, too. It sounds delicious."

"Will do." Dot headed to the back to start working on the orders.

"I wonder if Lucy, Ruth and Margaret will show up." They had told Gloria earlier in the week they were anxious to try Dot's new dish, too, but Gloria hadn't heard what time they planned to stop by.

She didn't have to wonder long as she spied Lucy's red head near the front door. Ruth was right behind her.

Gloria caught Ruth's eye and waved them over. "We should've taken the big table in the middle and sat together."

Paul, Gloria and the boys picked up their stuff and shifted it to the larger center table. There was still ample room for a couple more, just in case Margaret and her husband, Don, made an appearance.

Dot returned moments later with glasses of water for Ruth and Lucy and two large chocolate milkshakes for Ryan and Tyler.

Dot shifted the frosty glasses from the tray to the table.

"You're going to spoil those boys rotten," Gloria said.

Dot chuckled. "I think you've already taken care of that." She set the tray on the table, pulled out a chair and plopped down. "Margaret called earlier. She said Eleanor was willing to try the hypnosis."

Paul, who had just taken a sip of his water, swallowed wrong and began choking. "Hypnosis!" He turned to his wife. "You're going to try to hypnotize someone?"

Chapter 9

Tyler gulped his chocolate shake and wiped his mouth with the back of his shirtsleeve. "I wanna be hymnotized!"

"Hypnotized," Gloria corrected. "And I'm not the one doing it. Margaret is."

Paul rubbed his temple with his index and middle fingers. "Has she ever hypnotized anyone before?"

"Not that I know of," Dot answered. "But she's all jazzed up about it. Said she has been studying it online and thinks she can do it."

Ruth rested her elbows on the table. "This I gotta see."

"You can tomorrow," Gloria assured her. "She's going to Eleanor's house around ten tomorrow morning to try it."

"That's not fair," Ryan whined. "I wanna be hymnotized." He turned to his brother. "Let's try to hymnotize Mally when we get back to Grams."

"Yeah. You can sing hymns to Mally and put her to sleep," Gloria teased.

The group discussed the upcoming event in detail. Gloria couldn't see what it could possibly hurt. She'd started listening to a hypnotist's video earlier that day and it hadn't fazed her in the least. Of course, others might be more susceptible to the power of a hypnotist.

Honestly, Gloria didn't feel she knew enough about the subject...and neither did Margaret for that matter.

Their food...all-you-care-to-eat goulash for the adults, along with chili dogs and French fries for the boys, arrived a short time later.

Dot hovered nearby as the group tried their first spoonful of the thick, hearty stick-to-your-ribs-dish. "Well?"

Gloria tore a piece of crusty French bread from the end of her loaf, carved a small hole in the center and then scooped a heaping spoon full of goulash in the center. She popped the piece in her mouth.

The tangy sauce, mixed with large pieces of meat and seasonings Gloria couldn't quite put her finger on, exploded in a burst of flavor inside her mouth. "Delicious," she mumbled between chews. "Perfect."

She swallowed her food. "There's something in the goulash that gives it a wonderful, savory flavor."

Dot rattled off the ingredients. "Sautéed onion, green pepper, garlic, along with tomato paste, tomato sauce, diced tomatoes and meat with a sprinkle or two of Italian herb seasoning. That's about it."

"It's the combination of the garlic and green pepper, along with the onion," Gloria decided.

"I agree." Lucy scooped a spoonful in her mouth. "It's filling though. I'm not sure I'll have room for seconds."

Paul had already devoured half his bowl. "I'll make up for it," he promised.

The girls and Paul all agreed Dot had another hit on her hands.

The restaurant soon filled and Dot disappeared in the back as the orders poured in.

Gloria noted most of the diners ordered the goulash and many had seconds.

The conversation at the table shifted to Ed Mueller's death. "Did you hear Ed Mueller's wife, Sheryl, was here earlier today?" Ruth asked.

Gloria hadn't heard. She'd been too busy taking Mally to the vet, digging up the grate in the barn, which reminded her... She patted her front pants pocket and the small bulge. She had forgotten all about the button and coins the boys had found in the milking parlor drain.

"I heard Officer Joe Nelson was seen arguing with Ed Mueller out in front of the Quik Stop the other night." Gloria said.

"Judith Arnett told us that," Ruth reminded her.

"Right. Has anyone talked to Sally Keane yet?" Sally worked at the Quik Stop. Not only that, she had been dating Officer Joe Nelson on and off for the past year. The last Gloria had heard it was "off" again.

Lucy shook her head. "I haven't. Maybe Dot has." Sally ate at Dot's Restaurant once a week, like clockwork, on chicken 'n dumplings day.

Dot had just returned from the Quik Stop. Gloria wondered if Sally had been working.

"Well? Any seconds or thirds?" Dot returned to their table.

Paul leaned back in his chair and patted his stomach. "It was delicious, Dot, but I have to admit I am full."

She reached for his empty dish. "No dessert?"

"I'm afraid not," he said.

The boys had finished their dinner, too, leaving not a single scrap of food on their plates or a sip of chocolate shake in the bottom of the glasses.

Gloria, on the other hand, had a hard time finishing her bowl of goulash so Dot dropped off two to-go boxes – one of which was full of goulash.

Gloria scooped her leftovers in the empty container and snapped the lid shut. "Are you going to Eleanor's in the morning?"

"Ten you said?" Ruth reached for her purse, which was sitting next to her on the floor.

"Yep." Gloria nodded.

"I wouldn't miss it for the world," Lucy said.

Gloria rose from her chair while Paul made his way to the back to pay the bill. "I'll see you in the morning then."

She hugged Lucy, and then Ruth and watched them leave.

When Paul returned, the four of them headed to the car. During the ride home, the boys discussed how exactly they planned to hypnotize Mally.

When they reached the farm, the boys darted into the kitchen in search of their volunteer...err...guinea pig, Mally.

"C'mon Mally. Let's go in the living room," Ryan tugged on her collar. The boys and Mally disappeared into the living room.

Paul hung the car keys on the rack near the door and shrugged out of his jacket. "You're not concerned about Mally?"

"Nah!" Gloria waved a hand. "It'll be a miracle if they can get her to sit still long enough to wave anything in front of her eyes.

The boys found an old mood ring in the dining room hutch and they tied the ring to the end of a piece of string.

Gloria flipped a coin for who would try first. Tyler won the first round.

She quietly made her way to the living room doorway and peeked around the corner to watch.

Mally was sprawled out on the living room floor. Ryan and Tyler were sitting Indian style with their legs crossed, in front of her.

Tyler held the end of the string and slowly swung the mood ring back and forth. "You're getting very sleepy," he told Mally in a sing-song voice.

"Very sleepy," Ryan whispered.

"Shh," Tyler said and held his finger to his lips. "We can't both do this!"

Ryan clamped his mouth shut, crossed his arms and frowned.

Gloria pressed her hand to her mouth to keep from laughing.

Paul, who had crept up behind Gloria, peered over her shoulder and shook his head.

Mally tried to chomp down on the ring hanging from the string and then flopped back down on the carpeted floor, rolled over on her back and lifted her paws in the air.

Ryan rubbed her belly and shook her front paw.

Tyler threw the string and the ring on the floor. "You ruined it, Ryan. She was almost hymnotized."

"My turn." Ryan grabbed the string and held it up. As if on command, Mally rolled over and sat up. "Watch the ring Mally. Watch the ring swing back and forth, back and forth."

Mally, bored with the entire exercise, yawned and then shook herself before turning tail and heading into the dining room. She stopped next to Paul and Gloria for a quick greeting and then headed to the kitchen.

"I'm here." Gloria heard her daughter's cheery voice call out from the kitchen.

Tyler picked up the ring and handed it to his grandmother before Ryan and he raced to the kitchen and over to their mother who stood near the door. "We found some old money and a button in the barn," Ryan announced as he hugged his mother.

"And a spiddune," Tyler added.

"A spittoon that must have belonged to your grandparents or great grandparents," Gloria said.

Jill kissed the top of Ryan's head. "You did? Are the coins valuable?"

Once again, Gloria had forgotten about the coins and the button. She reached in her front pocket and pulled them out.

She plucked the button from the small pile in the palm of her hand and handed it to her daughter. "This is an old button from a pair of overalls that once belonged to your dad or grandfather."

Jill narrowed her eyes and studied the button. "You don't say." She turned it over in her hand. "Oh my gosh! I remember Grandpa Rutherford wearing those old bib overalls." She looked up. "They were blue denim with a large pocket in the front." She pointed to the top of her chest. "Right here."

Jill smiled. "He used to roll the pant legs up and wear a button down shirt with a white t-shirt underneath. I always wondered if he had only one outfit since he seemed to be wearing the same thing every time I saw him."

"Remember the goofy hat?" Gloria asked. The hat was an old denim hat - part beanie and part train conductor. He wore it pushed back on his forehead and Gloria wondered why he even bothered since it never protected his face from the blistering summer sun.

Gloria took the button from her daughter and placed it near the center of the kitchen table, out of Mally's reach. She handed Jill the coins. "I haven't had a chance to clean these up and take a good look at them."

She shifted her gaze to her grandsons. "If they're worth any money, I'll let you know," she promised them.

Ryan hopped up and down. "I hope they're worth a bazillion dollars and I can buy all kinds of video games."

"Mally threw up," Tyler told his mom.

Jill frowned. "Is Mally sick?"

"No. The boys ran their metal detector over Mally and it went off. We were missing a leather key ring. Long story short, we paid a visit to the vet today. He took an x-ray and found she had swallowed the key ring."

Tyler picked up the story. "So we stopped at the store and picked up some gross stuff for Mally to eat. Then she threw up and I found the key ring."

"Me too," Ryan insisted.

"She's fine," Gloria said.

The boys slipped their feet into their boots and pulled their coats on.

Jill leaned over and hugged her mother. "Thanks for watching them, Mom. No wonder they beg to come over here all the time. Your house is much more exciting than ours."

Mally darted into the yard for an evening patrol and Gloria, Jill and the boys followed her out.

"Grams is the best," Ryan said. He reached over and wrapped his arms around Gloria's waist, nearly knocking her off balance.

"Careful," Jill warned.

Tyler hugged his grandmother a little more gently and Paul followed them out, carrying their metal detectors.

The boys promised Gloria they would take care of the detectors and would bring them back when they next visited so they could thoroughly search the rest of the farm.

Paul and Gloria waited until Jill backed the car out of the drive and turned onto the road before closing the porch door and locking it.

Gloria leaned against the door and gazed at her husband. "Whew! It feels as if I just escaped a whirlwind."

Chapter 10

Gloria jerked as the alarm clock jarred her awake. She reached out and fumbled with the clock to shut it off.

She had tossed and turned all night, mulling over poor Ed Mueller's death, worrying that the longer she waited to start poking around for clues and talking to the suspects, the colder the trail grew.

Paul would be busy working his security detail for the next couple of days, which would give Gloria plenty of time to ramp up the investigation.

The first thing she planned to do was stop by the Quik Stop before heading to Eleanor's place. She hoped Sally Keane was working. Plus, she needed to stock up on chips and sliced cheddar cheese, not to mention pop. The boys had wiped out Paul and Gloria's snack shelf.

She wondered how much her daughter, Jill, spent on groceries feeding the growing boys. A lot more than Paul and she spent.

After she stopped by the store, it would be time to head to Eleanor's house for Margaret's hypnosis experiment. Gloria secretly thought it a waste of time, but Margaret seemed confident it would work.

Perhaps Margaret would prove her wrong and the exercise would jog Eleanor's memory. Either way, it would be entertaining.

Dot had called the night before to tell her Ray promised to hold down the fort at the restaurant so she could come, too. She offered to bring an array of tasty treats and Gloria told her she would bring plates and napkins.

She wondered if the police had finished searching the Mueller's cottage and then remembered she had unlocked one of the cottage's bedroom windows, just in case she needed to get back inside.

Gloria shifted on the mattress and adjusted her broken leg. If she decided to "take a look around," she would have to take someone with her. There was no way she could climb through the bedroom window.

Paul crawled out of bed first. "I'll go get ready."

Gloria threw back the covers and swung her legs off the bed.

Mally was waiting at the end of the bed for someone to let her outside. "Might as well get this day under way."

She hobbled to the kitchen and opened the door to let Mally out before shuffling over to the coffee pot.

Gloria dumped a heaping mound of coffee in the filter, filled the reservoir with water and turned the machine on.

While the coffee brewed, Gloria scrambled a few eggs, fried several slices of bacon, adding a few extra pieces for Mally and Puddles, her cat, who watched her every move.

Mally, who had returned from a trip outside, settled in next to Puddles and both were patiently waiting for tasty treats.

Paul made his way into the kitchen, grabbed a plate and filled it with food. He made a second one for Gloria and then carried both to the table.

"Meow." Puddles circled the legs of Gloria's chair.

"I'm working on it," she told her beloved pets as she placed a small pile of eggs in the center of two paper plates, added a small amount of bacon to each and then set both plates on the floor.

Paul watched in silence. "Those are two lucky pets, right there," he commented as he reached for his fork. "Which reminds me, how is At Your Service doing?"

Gloria told him that Alice had asked her to stop by At Your Service when she had a chance. They had just matched one of their dogs with a young boy who had lost his hearing at a young age and they had videotaped the meeting.

"Maybe we should run by there this weekend," Paul suggested.

"I may go today, but if not, we can go together," Gloria said.

"Speaking of plans, what are you up to today?"

"I'm going to run to the Quik Stop to pick up a few things and then head to Eleanor's for Margaret's hypnosis session."

"Huh." Paul wasn't convinced that was *all* Gloria was up to, but decided not to press the issue.

He chewed his last bite of toast, wiped his mouth and dropped the dirty napkin on top. Paul cleared the table while Gloria filled a travel thermos with coffee.

She followed him to the door and waited for him to slip into his jacket and grab his truck keys.

"I have my suspicions you're up to something else." Paul wrapped his arms around his wife and pulled her close. "Try to stay out of trouble today."

Gloria lifted her face and Paul kissed his wife. "I'll do my best."

She held the door open and watched as he stepped off the porch, walked down the sidewalk and climbed into his truck. She waited for him to pull onto the road before closing the door.

"Time to get this show on the road!"

***

Gloria had just enough time to make a stop by the Quik Stop to pick up a few items before heading to Eleanor's house.

She cast a glance skyward at the gathering storm clouds.

Gloria caught the last few minutes of the morning forecast and knew the snow would soon start falling, followed by strong gusty winds. Near white out conditions were headed their way.

The full force of the storm wasn't supposed to reach Belhaven until mid-afternoon, unless, of course, forecasters were wrong. Gloria planned to be back home and safely inside before the first snowflake hit the ground.

She pulled Annabelle into an empty parking spot in front of the grocery store, shuffled onto the sidewalk and hobbled to the store door. Once inside, she cast a glance at the checkout counter. It was empty.

Gloria shifted her gaze to the back of the store and the new deli display case where she caught a glimpse of Sally's curly brown hair.

She plucked a hand basket from the stack and made a beeline for the back of the store.

"Hi Sally."

Sally's head popped up. "Good Morning Gloria. I see you're here early. Trying to beat the snowstorm?"

"Something like that," Gloria replied. "I would like a half pound of corned beef and a half pound of smoked turkey."

Sally nodded and opened the back of the display case. "I hope Brian lets me leave work early if this storm blows up like the forecasters are predicting. The tires on my car are almost bald and the last time I got caught on slippery roads I almost ended up in the ditch."

Gloria had almost forgotten Sally's penchant for complaining...all the time. She interrupted Sally's rant. "Did you hear about the poor unfortunate summer resident, Ed Mueller?"

Sally nodded as she bagged the corned beef and placed the bag on top of the scale. She pulled the sticker from the machine and slapped it on the side of the bag before handing it to Gloria. "Terrible tragedy. Why, can you imagine being trapped in the ice, unable to save yourself? What a horrible way to die."

"No kidding." Gloria placed the packet of corned beef in her basket. "I caught a glimpse of poor Ed's body. You have to wonder how in the world he got trapped in the ice."

Sally grabbed a set of tongs and plucked a pile of smoked turkey from the display tray. "Ed stopped in here to pick up some trash bags the evening before his body was found. Said he was doing a little cleaning at the cottage and then heading home later that night."

Chapter 11

Sally rattled on, but Gloria's mind was stuck on what she'd just said. Ed Mueller had not intended to spend the night at the cottage, which made sense. The wood stove was cold.

Why would he make a special trip to Belhaven just to "clean up" around the cottage, and then turn around and leave? Why not come for the weekend or at the very least, plan on spending the night?

Her sleuthing radar shifted into high gear. What could he possibly have planned to "clean"? Was he trying to hide something...possibly from his wife? Her gut told her Ed Mueller's trip to Belhaven was directly related to his death.

Were Ed and Sheryl Mueller involved in some sort of crime?

Gloria opened her mouth to ask if Sally would agree it was odd, but quickly clamped it shut. She remembered a while back Sally spreading a rumor that Gloria was creating mysteries just so she could be in the spotlight.

The thought made her ears burn. She pushed aside her sudden anger and forced a smile.

Sally handed her the package of smoked turkey. "Can I get you anything else?"

Gloria took the packet from Sally. "No. I have a couple small items to grab on my way to the checkout counter."

She hobbled through the chip aisle; passed on the soda pop since she had no idea how she could juggle a 12-pack of soda along with the other purchases, and headed to the front of the store.

Sally rang up Gloria's purchases, placed them in plastic grocery sacks and slid them across the counter. "Joe told me investigators suspect foul play." She lowered her voice, although they were the only two in the front of the store. "I think the wife was involved. He was a player, you know."

Gloria nodded, but didn't reply. She slid the handles of the bags onto her arm and adjusted her crutches. "I hope you make it home before the storm hits."

Sally rolled her eyes. "For heaven's sake, I sure hope so."

Gloria shifted around and hobbled to the exit.

The door swung open just as she reached for the handle, causing Gloria to jerk backward and almost lose her balance.

A woman with cropped gray locks, steely gray eyes and scarecrow thin figure burst through the door.

It was Lynda Clemson, another of the part-time summer residents. She and her husband, Ben, owned the cottage next door to the Mueller's cottage. Lynda attended the Church of God during the summer months when she was in town.

Gloria hadn't seen her since the fall festival back in October.

Lynda reached forward to steady Gloria. "Oh my gosh! I am so sorry Gloria!" She gazed at Gloria's cast. "What in the world happened to you?" she gasped.

Gloria sucked in a breath and shook her head. "It's a long story. Nice to see you Lynda."

Lynda Clemson waited until Gloria had cleared the doorway and was safely on the sidewalk before she closed the front door to the grocery store.

The winter winds had picked up and Gloria shivered as she tucked the collar of her coat around her neck. A snowflake hit the tip of her nose and she stared up at the snow clouds. "I thought you were holding off until later," she scowled.

Even though the snow had begun to fall, it would take several hours before the roads became treacherous. A snowflake or two wasn't going to kill her.

On the other hand, the thought of icy sidewalks and roads, combined with her crutches and cast made her nervous.

Gloria opened the driver's side door, gave the bag of groceries a light toss, grabbed the top of the doorframe and shoved her crutches into the passenger seat. "I'm going to have a bonfire and burn these babies as soon as this cast comes off," she promised herself as she slid into the driver's seat.

When she reached Eleanor's place, Margaret's SUV, Dot's van and Lucy's jeep were already in the drive. Andrea pulled in behind her and Gloria spotted Ruth in the passenger seat. It was apparent no one wanted to miss Margaret's hypnosis experiment.

Lucy must have been on the lookout for Gloria because she darted down Eleanor's front steps and met Gloria near the driver's side door. She reached across Gloria and grabbed her crutches. "You bought groceries?"

Gloria reached for the paper plates and napkins. She hopped out of the car and took the crutches from Lucy. "I picked up a few things but they'll be fine in the car. It's cold enough." She shoved a crutch under each arm and trailed behind Lucy as they made their way to the front steps.

She handed the crutches to Lucy, grabbed the handrail and hopped up the first step, then the second and finally the third.

"You're getting to be an expert at balancing on one foot," Lucy remarked.

"It's a skill I can live without," Gloria quipped. She hopped into the empty living room. The chatter of excited voices echoed from the kitchen. "She hasn't started yet, has she?"

"No," Lucy said as she handed Gloria her crutches. "Margaret is chomping at the bit but we made her wait until everyone got here."

Andrea and Ruth followed them inside.

Lucy fell in step with Gloria and the foursome made their way into the kitchen. "Who ate my pink frosted sprinkle donut?" Lucy demanded.

"No one." Dot laughed. "It's over there on top of the microwave."

The girls made room for the new arrivals and Dot shifted a chair sideways so Gloria could sit down.

Andrea poured a cup of coffee and slid it in front of Gloria while Dot placed Gloria's favorite donut, a chocolate éclair, on a paper plate and set it in front of her. "You guys are spoiling me. I may have to keep the crutches awhile longer."

Ruth snorted. "The way you're moaning and groaning about the broken leg cramping your style, I don't think so."

Gloria broke the chocolate éclair in half and licked the creamy center. "True," she admitted. "It's driving me crazy."

"As long as the cast is off before the cruise," Margaret said. "Speaking of cruise, someone said Liz and Frances are booked on the same ship and in a suite near us."

"Yeah. When she heard we were going on a girls' cruise, she got on the horn with Lucy, who told her where and when we were going and even helped her check for available cabins." Gloria gave Lucy a dark look.

Lucy shrugged her shoulders. "What? Did you want me to lie?"

"It's a thought," Gloria sighed. "Bottom line is France and Liz are across the hall from our suites. I'm pretty sure they plan on driving down the night before and staying at the same hotel."

"This ought to be exciting," Dot commented.

Andrea peeled the wrapper off her blueberry muffin. "Is she really that bad? I mean, she seemed all right when I met her."

The group groaned in unison.

"You have no idea." Margaret grinned and patted Gloria's hand. "Don't worry. We'll protect you from big, bad sis."

Eleanor swiped the last smear of chocolate frosting from her plate with her index finger and then licked it off. "Do you think this hypnosis thing will work?"

All eyes shifted to Margaret, who squirmed at being the center of attention. "I-I don't know," she confessed. "I hope so. All we can do is try."

After the group finished devouring the delicious goodies Dot had brought with her, Margaret grabbed a dishrag from the sink and wiped the crumbs from the table.

"Before I forget, I stopped by the Quik Stop this morning and Sally Keane said the day before Ed Mueller died, he had stopped by the store to buy a box of trash bags."

"And?" Lucy leaned in.

"He told her he wasn't staying overnight but was only in town long enough to do a little cleaning at the cottage."

"That explains why the wood stove was cold," Eleanor commented.

Margaret slapped an open palm on the tabletop. "All the more reason to find out what clue is lurking in the back of Eleanor's head."

She unbuttoned the cuff of her sleeves and rolled them up. "It's time to get down to business!"

Chapter 12

Gloria still had her misgivings about the whole "hypnosis" mumbo-jumbo, but didn't want to hurt Margaret's feelings since she seemed certain it would help Eleanor remember exactly what she had seen at the Mueller's cottage the night before Ed Mueller's body had been found in the lake.

They would be much better off praying to God for help in solving the case but she held her tongue.

Margaret pulled an iPad from her purse, turned it on and set it on the table, placing it between Eleanor and her.

A man's droning voice began to speak. "Take a slow, deep breath and hold it in…and now let it out. Just breathe deeply and slowly as you allow your body and mind to relax."

Gloria rolled her eyes.

Lucy snorted.

Andrea covered her mouth to keep from laughing.

Eleanor took a deep breath.

The monotone voice continued. "Make sure that you're sitting down or even lying down in a comfortable position..."

"Clear the deck!" With the swipe of her arm, Margaret sent the center table doily along with the salt and pepper shakers sailing across the table.

Lucy lunged, catching the shaker of salt midair. "Got it."

"Nice catch," Andrea said.

Margaret patted the tabletop. "Here, lie down on the table," she told Eleanor.

"What in the world," Gloria muttered.

"That can't be comfortable," Dot objected.

Margaret ignored the others as she grasped Eleanor under her right elbow. When she was standing upright, she motioned Lucy to help her ease Eleanor onto the flat, butcher-block surface. "It's only for a few minutes."

Margaret pressed the stop button on the recording and settled Eleanor on the table. "Give me your sweater." She snapped her fingers and pointed at the sweater Ruth was wearing.

Ruth removed her sweater. "Good grief." She handed it to Margaret who rolled it up and slid it under Eleanor's head.

Eleanor glanced at the five faces staring at her and squeezed her eyes shut as she folded her hands and placed them on her stomach.

Margaret pressed the play button on the iPad.

"Continue breathing in and out until your breaths become slow and even...allow your mind to drift..."

The recording droned on.

Eleanor's hands fell to her sides.

Gloria leaned in, looking for signs that Eleanor was still breathing. "I think you killed her," she said.

Eleanor shifted slightly and began to snore softly.

Lucy burst out laughing.

Margaret frowned and paused the recording. "She wasn't supposed to fall asleep!"

They all stared at the sleeping woman. Now that Gloria studied her closely, she didn't look too uncomfortable.

"I should borrow the recording," Ruth said. "I haven't been sleeping well lately."

Margaret gave her a dark look. "Well, at least I had an idea. We're back to square one!"

Eleanor snorted and flopped sideways. She opened one eye and peered at the women. "D-did I just fall asleep?"

Gloria smiled and nodded. "So much for hypnosis." Dot and she helped Eleanor slide off the kitchen table.

Eleanor patted Margaret's arm. "At least you tried." She pulled her walker close and then shuffled over to the kitchen sink. "Would anyone like more coffee or tea?"

The girls shook their head. "No thanks," Andrea said.

"That's it!" Eleanor exclaimed.

All eyes shifted to Eleanor.

She turned to face the girls seated at the table. "I remembered what I saw the other night!"

"See? It worked!" Margaret beamed triumphantly.

"No!" Eleanor shook her head. She pointed to window in front of the kitchen sink. "Officer Joe Nelson's patrol car is parked at Mueller's cottage. I saw his vehicle there the night before Ed Mueller was found frozen in the lake!"

Gloria jumped out of her seat and ran to the window. She leaned over Eleanor's shoulder for a glimpse of the Mueller's cottage. Sure enough, a Montbay County Sheriff's patrol car was parked in the drive.

Eleanor and Gloria watched as Officer Joe Nelson strolled to his patrol car. He glanced around, and then looked directly at Eleanor's place.

Gloria jerked back, hoping he hadn't caught a glimpse of her.

Eleanor waved.

"I hope he didn't see us," Gloria muttered.

Eleanor put her hand down. "Why not? Officer Joe is such a nice young man."

"Because Officer Joe is a suspect," Gloria said. "Someone spotted him arguing with Ed Mueller the night before his body was found in the lake."

Gloria hobbled over to the table, passing by the sliding glass doors on her way.

The police patrol car was driving up the hill. She leaned forward and watched as he turned down Eleanor's street and slowly drove by her house.

As quickly as she could, Gloria limped to the living room picture window that faced the street. She lifted the edge of the curtain and watched his patrol car stop at the corner.

Suddenly, the lights flashed and the sound of a police siren echoed, followed by the squeal of tires as his patrol car quickly disappeared from sight.

The other Garden Girls had followed Gloria into the living room and peeked through the curtains.

Lucy stared over Gloria's shoulder. "I wonder what he was doing at the Mueller's cottage."

Gloria shifted to the side. "I don't know but I think it's time to do a little recon."

"Recon?" Eleanor asked.

"Reconnaissance," Gloria explained.

Eleanor shook her head.

"Snoop," Margaret said bluntly.

Ruth rubbed her hands together. "Now?"

"Now would be the perfect time, what with Officer Joe heading in the other direction." Gloria gazed at Dot. "We need someone to drop us off in front of the Mueller's cottage."

Dot pointed at her chest. "Me?" she squeaked. Dot tried her best to stay on the sidelines during Gloria's investigations. She was more of a behind-the-scenes member of the group.

To be the designated driver of the getaway car, or in her case, van, was better suited for one of the other more adventurous girls...at least that was her opinion.

Lucy patted Dot's shoulder. "Don't worry. All you have to do is drop us off in front of the cottage and then wait for one of us to call you to come pick us up."

Dot ran a hand through her hair. "I-I..."

"Good," Gloria interrupted. She turned to Eleanor. "Do you have any rubber gloves we could borrow and maybe a flashlight? We don't want to leave prints, just in case investigators aren't finished."

Eleanor nodded and scooted back to the kitchen. She returned moments later with the requested items inside the basket attached to the front of her walker.

Gloria took the two flashlights and box of latex gloves.

"I have a few black ski masks if you want," Eleanor offered.

Gloria was about to ask what in the world Eleanor was doing with black ski masks but changed her mind. Some things were better left alone. This was one of them. "Ready?"

Ruth opened the front door while Eleanor, followed by Andrea, Lucy, Margaret, a reluctant Dot, and last but not least, Gloria, made their way down the steps and over to Dot's van.

"If I get arrested, someone better bail me out," Dot said.

"Paul will bail us out," Gloria reassured her friend. Although he would probably let her sit and stew in a jail cell to teach her a lesson. She shrugged. It wouldn't be the first time.

The girls climbed into the van and Dot hopped behind the wheel. "Here goes nothing."

Chapter 13

Dot backed out of the drive and pulled onto the road. When she reached the corner, she stopped, looked both ways and pressed on the gas. "When I stop the van, you need to hurry and jump out so no one sees you," she said nervously as she gripped the steering wheel.

Lucy laughed. "Gloria is on crutches and Eleanor has a walker. I'm not sure how fast we're gonna be."

"If we try to move too fast, it will look suspicious," Margaret pointed out.

"You don't think five women climbing out of a van and descending on a dead man's cottage will look suspicious?" Andrea asked.

The van had reached the bottom of the hill and slowed to a stop in front of the Mueller's gravel drive.

Gloria reached for the van's door handle. "It's the middle of the afternoon. Most of these cottages are vacant so I doubt anyone will spot us."

Dot hit the brakes. "Go! Go! Go!"

Ruth was the last to exit the van. "We'll call when we're ready." She pulled the door shut and followed the other girls, who were hustling past the side door of the house. She caught up with them near the back deck slider.

Andrea studied the exterior of the cottage. "How are we going to get in?"

Gloria hobbled over to the bedroom window she had unlocked the other day...before Officer Joe Nelson caught Eleanor, Andrea and her inside the house and told them they had to leave. She hoped no one had noticed and that the window was still unlocked.

She slid her finger in the crook and pulled up. The window silently slid open and Gloria let out the breath she'd been holding.

Her relief was short-lived. On closer inspection, the window was much smaller than she remembered.

Gloria turned her head and studied the group of women hovering nearby. *Margaret?* Nope. She remembered their trip to the Smoky Mountains. There was no way Margaret would crawl through the small window.

Eleanor was automatically disqualified, although she appeared eager and willing.

Next was Ruth. Ruth was a real team player but somehow she couldn't visualize her friend's ample frame fitting through the narrow opening. Visions of Ruth getting stuck in the window and them having to call the fire department to rescue her filled Gloria's mind.

"Lucy or Andrea. Which one of you wants to crawl through the window and unlock the back door?" Gloria asked.

"Me," they both answered in unison.

Andrea turned to Lucy. "We can go together."

The girls slipped their rubber gloves on and Andrea stepped over to the open window.

"Here. I'll give you a leg up." Lucy cupped her hands together and bent down.

Andrea placed the heel of her sneaker in the palm of Lucy's hands.

"Heave-ho," Lucy said as Andrea pulled and Lucy pushed her through the open window.

After Andrea was safely inside, Ruth stepped forward to help Lucy but Lucy waved her off. "Nah! I got this one." She easily lifted herself onto the frame and quickly disappeared inside. Her head reappeared moments later. "Meet us at the side door. Lucy pulled the window shut.

Eleanor, Ruth, Margaret and Gloria made their way over to the back porch door.

The door swung open. "This place smells funny," Andrea said as they stepped inside.

Gloria sniffed the air. She was right. The interior of the cottage had a unique odor. The other day it had smelled musty but today there was a different smell...a smell she couldn't quite put her finger on. "I agree. It smells..."

"Gross." Margaret wrinkled her nose.

Gloria pulled the small pile of latex gloves from her front coat pocket and handed a pair to the girls, who quickly slipped them on.

"What are we looking for?" Ruth asked as she wiggled her fingers and tugged the snug gloves on.

"Anything odd or unusual. Notes, blood stains, weapons, the standard stuff," Gloria said as she hopped to the bathroom.

"Drugs," Eleanor quipped.

"Drugs," Gloria agreed. "Just put your detective cap on."

Ruth and Andrea headed to the bedroom. Eleanor started in the kitchen while Margaret started poking around in the living room. Lucy helped Margaret search the living room.

Gloria hobbled to the bathroom and opened the medicine cabinet above the sink. Inside the cabinet was a disposable razor, a box of Band-Aids, some sunscreen and dental floss.

She scooted back and opened the cabinet under the sink, which was full of towels, washcloths, some toilet bowl cleaner and a half-empty bottle of shampoo.

The only thing left was the shower. She swiped the shower curtain to the side and stuck her head inside the shower. It was empty, except for a bar of soap on the shelf and a back scrubber hanging from the showerhead.

She hobbled into the living room where Margaret had just replaced the living room sofa cushion. "Clean as a whistle," she said.

"Same here," Andrea agreed.

"Phew!" Eleanor gasped as she leaned over the kitchen trashcan. "I think I found the putrid odor!"

"What is it?" Gloria made her way over to the garbage and inched close to Eleanor. Inside the can were several dead fish, still intact. "Why would someone toss perfectly good fish into the garbage can?"

Most of the area fishermen would toss smaller fish back into the water. Catch and release. These were smallmouth bass and not small at all.

Ruth moved forward and peeked inside. She clamped her hand across her mouth and began to gag.

Andrea waved her hand across her face and took a step back. The rotting smell quickly filled the cottage.

"Close the lid!" Margaret gasped.

Eleanor started to shut the lid when something caught Gloria's eye. She held her hand out. "Wait! I see something!"

Gloria reached inside with her gloved hand and pulled out a tag, a nametag to be exact. She read the name on the tag aloud. "Sally Keane."

Chapter 14

Gloria's cell phone, which was tucked in her front jacket pocket, began ringing. She pulled it out, turned it over and stared at the screen. It was Dot.

She turned it to speaker and hit answer. "Hello?"

"You gotta get out of there!" Dot shrieked. "I just saw Officer Joe Nelson's patrol car pass by Eleanor's house!"

Eleanor dropped the lid on the trashcan.

Andrea raced to the door and threw it open.

Ruth bolted out, followed by Margaret, then Lucy. Gloria, unwilling to leave any man...err...woman behind, waited for Eleanor to shuffle out of the cottage.

She closed the door behind Eleanor, making sure she had locked it before picking up the pace or in her case, the hobble, as she hurried to Dot's waiting van, which was parked at the end of the drive.

By the time she made it to the van, the others were already inside. Andrea was near the door waving frantically. "Hurry! Dot said she spotted his patrol car coming down the hill!"

Lucy reached out and grabbed the top of Gloria's jacket, yanking her inside the van just as Dot stomped on the gas, spraying loose gravel in the air as she sped off down the road.

"Agh!" Andrea, seeing Gloria's legs still hanging out the side of the open van door, gave Lucy a helping hand as they both tugged on their friend's arm, pulling Gloria the rest of the way in.

Lucy rolled the door shut. "We're in!"

Gloria flipped from her stomach to her back and sat upright. "Barely!"

When Dot reached the end of the cul-de-sac, she circled around and headed back down the road.

The police patrol car was coming from the opposite direction now, and he slowed when Dot's van got close.

Dot glanced in the rearview mirror at her accomplices. "Hit the floor so he doesn't see you!"

The girls flattened themselves against the floor of the van.

The officer rolled down his driver's side window and motioned for Dot to stop.

"He wants me to stop," Dot groaned.

Gloria closed her eyes. "Please God. Help Dot say the right thing and not blow our cover."

"H-hello Officer Joe," Dot stuttered after she hit the brakes and lowered the van window.

The sound of Officer Joe Nelson's voice drifted in through the open window. Gloria was only able to catch a few words. "...place...lunch...warning."

"Yes, I know." Dot laughed nervously. "I promise I won't let Gloria suck me into anything, either."

Gloria frowned and lifted her head. What was the officer telling her?

Lucy pointed at Gloria and silently laughed to which Gloria gave her a death look.

"Okay. Good-bye." Dot rolled up the window and the van began to move. "He said he suspects Gloria is sticking her nose in where it doesn't belong," she said.

"Well, maybe if he did his job, I wouldn't have to do it for him," Gloria said as she shifted to a sitting position.

Ruth patted her arm. "Don't worry. There's only a handful of people in Belhaven who think you stick your nose in where it doesn't belong."

If Ruth was trying to make Gloria feel better, it wasn't working.

"I-I..." Gloria paused. Did her friends and neighbors think she was a busybody? She always thought she was helping others.

Eleanor squeezed her hand. "I pulled you into this investigation," she reminded her. "Remember? I called you."

"And I'm the one who wanted to try hypnotizing Eleanor," Margaret added.

Lucy swiped a stray strand of hair from her eyes. "We're all in this together. You haven't twisted anyone's arm."

"That's right," Andrea agreed. "I think Officer Joe Nelson is involved somehow. I mean, he has been lurking around the Mueller's cottage ever since Ed Mueller's body was found."

Gloria reached into her front coat pocket and pulled Sally Keane's nametag out. Could it be Sally Keane was somehow involved in Ed Mueller's death and the cop was trying to cover something up to save Sally's hide?

What did Sally mean when she said Ed Mueller was a "player?" Had he been messing around with another woman, his wife had somehow found out and then she killed him?

She told the girls about her conversation with Sally.

"Maybe his wife did him in," Lucy theorized.

"What about Officer Joe Nelson?" Gloria asked. "Motive and opportunity. He may have found out about a clandestine affair between Ed and Sally. The two were spotted arguing the night before his death. Maybe he killed him and put his body in the shanty."

Margaret added her own theory. "Or Sally was a scorned woman and she poisoned him and then dumped him in the lake."

Dot parked her van behind Gloria's car and the women hopped out of the back.

Gloria glanced at her watch. "I better head home. First, I'll have to take the nametag to Montbay County Sheriff's station to turn it in as evidence." She briefly wondered what she would tell the police when she got there.

The women all climbed into their cars but first agreed to meet up for breakfast at Dot's Restaurant the next morning to mull over the day's events.

Gloria wiggled into the driver's seat, slid her crutches onto the passenger seat and pulled the door shut.

It was less than half an hour drive to Montbay County Sheriff's station in nearby Langstone.

When she got to the police station, Gloria steered Annabelle into an empty spot on the street and shuffled across the road to the front entrance.

She hobbled up the steps and entered the lobby, which was all too familiar. The girl behind the counter was the same one Gloria had met on her first visit to Montbay County sheriff's police station. It seemed like an eternity ago.

The girl smiled as Gloria approached the counter. "Hello Mrs. Kennedy. Congratulations on your recent marriage to Officer Kennedy."

Gloria smiled. "Thank you."

"I heard you had quite an exciting honeymoon."

Gloria frowned. Had Paul been going around telling his buddies about his new wife's mishaps?

"Officer Joe Nelson said you broke your leg chasing after a peeping tom."

Her frown deepened. Was the man a blabbermouth like his girlfriend, Sally Keane? Gloria vowed to watch what she said around Officer Joe Nelson. "Yes, and thank goodness the cast is coming off soon."

She went on. "I was hoping to talk with the person in charge of the Ed Mueller investigation. He was the man whose body was found on Lake Terrace."

"That would be Stan Woszinski, Officer Kennedy's former partner. Let me see if he's still here." The young woman popped out of her chair and disappeared down the hall.

Gloria propped her crutches against the counter and balanced on her uninjured leg. She was getting good at balancing and was sometimes able to get around with only one crutch.

"Follow me."

The clerk stood in the doorway and motioned Gloria to follow.

Gloria grabbed both crutches and trailed behind the quick moving girl, who stopped abruptly in front of a familiar door. It was the door to Paul's office...old office.

She shifted to the side and peered around the corner.

"Gloria Kennedy." A grinning Officer Stan Woszinski scooched to the front of his chair and stood. "Jen said you had something on the Mueller case. Have a seat, have a seat."

Gloria nodded and settled into the chair closest to the door. "I...my friends and I were inside the Mueller cottage earlier today and kind of..."

Officer Woszinski eased into his chair and crossed his arms. "Did the owner let you in?" he interrupted.

"Technically – no. We kind of let ourselves in."

"So you broke into a dead man's cottage searching for clues."

Woszinski rubbed the stubble on his chin. "I could arrest you and your friends if the owner wanted to press charges," he told her.

Stan Woszinski was one tough cookie. He wasn't cutting Gloria any slack and the way he stared at her warned he might do exactly that!

"I...we didn't mean any harm. We were just trying to help," she said. Looking back, perhaps she should've gone to Officer Joe Nelson with the nametag, although she still considered him a prime suspect.

Gloria quickly changed the subject as she pulled the plastic tag from her coat pocket and placed it on the desk. "We found this in Ed Mueller's trashcan near the door. It was under some rotting fish."

Stan leaned forward, reached across the desk and picked up the nametag. He turned it over and his eyes narrowed.

Gloria was one hundred percent certain Officer Woszinski recognized the name. Sally and Officer Joe Nelson had been an item for several months and had even attended Paul and Gloria's wedding as a couple. Officer Woszinski and his wife had been there too.

Woszinski lifted his gaze. "Did you find anything else?"

Gloria shook her head. "No, we didn't. I know your officers thoroughly investigated the crime scene, but wondered if they, too, noticed the wood stove inside the Mueller cottage was cold the morning his body was found, which meant either Ed Mueller hadn't had time to light the stove or hadn't planned to stay at the cottage."

The officer nodded noncommittally as he grabbed a pen and began jotting notes on a yellow pad in front of him. "So you were in the Mueller cottage more than once."

Was he building a case to have her arrested? Gloria's heart began to pound. She rubbed her damp palms on top of her pants. "The door was open and we left as soon as the police told us to go."

"We? How many people are we talking about?"

"Only a couple. Three or four. Maybe five. Somewhere in there." She waved a dismissive hand.

Officer Woszinski stopped writing and set the pen on top of the pad. "Just between you and me, you could have gotten into a lot of trouble, but Paul is my friend and I'm gonna cut you some slack and let you off with a verbal warning."

Gloria knew what was coming next. She shrank back in the chair.

"Stay out of this investigation. Montbay County Sheriff's investigative team is on this case. Leave it to the professionals Gloria. There's a killer still out there on the loose."

Officer Woszinski tapped his fingertips on the desk. "Have you ever thought what might happen if the killer finds out you're snooping around? You're putting your life and the lives of your friends in danger."

He abruptly stood.

Gloria, taking this as her cue to leave, stood.

"I'll walk you out."

She followed him down the hall, into the lobby and then out the front door. "No wonder Paul retired. Keeping you out of trouble must be a full time job."

Gloria opened her mouth to reply and then promptly shut it. She wasn't about to look a gift horse in the mouth. At least he wasn't going to arrest her for tampering with evidence, although, in her opinion, she wasn't tampering. She was the one who had found the nametag!

Gloria stepped onto the sidewalk. She balanced her purse on her arm and adjusted her crutches. "Here goes nothing!" She quickly hobbled across the busy street.

When she safely reached the other side, she leaned against the car and waited for a line of traffic to pass by before quickly unlocking her door and slipping inside. "Well, that was fun," she mumbled as she started the car and pulled onto the road.

She had made it into the town of Belhaven and turned onto the road leading toward the farm when her cell phone began ringing.

She pulled off to the side of the road and reached inside her purse, pulling it out. It was Margaret. "Hello?"

"Listen, I know you're probably on your way home from the police station but wondered if you could stop by my place first. I have an idea."

Chapter 15

Gloria wanted to go home. A dull ache had begun to radiate from the bottom of her kneecap all the way down to the tips of her toes.

When the girls jerked her into the van earlier, it had jarred her broken bone, although she couldn't blame them for pulling her in. It was either that or be caught red-handed by the officer.

Her curiosity to find out exactly what "idea" Margaret had in mind outweighed the dull ache. "I'm on my way. I need an aspirin."

"I'll have one waiting for you when you get here."

Margaret was standing in the breezeway entrance when Gloria pulled in the drive. She held the door open and waited for Gloria to hobble around the side of the car and into the house.

The wind had picked up and the smattering of snowflakes had turned into a steady snowfall. She gazed up at the sky as she stepped inside. "The storm is getting closer."

Margaret nodded and closed the door behind her. "Ruth said she heard Ed Mueller was stabbed with an ice pick."

"An ice pick?" That would be a bloody crime scene. Maybe that was why someone had covered him with a blanket from the chin down.

When Gloria reached the kitchen, Margaret handed her a glass of water and two aspirin. Gloria popped the aspirin in her mouth and gulped the water. She set the half-empty water glass on the counter. "Whatcha got?"

"Well, I was thinking. Follow me." She motioned Gloria through the kitchen toward the back of the house and to the rear patio sliders that faced the lake...Lake Terrace.

Margaret unlocked the slider and stepped onto the snowy deck. "You can almost see Ed Mueller's shanty from here."

Gloria shifted to the right and gazed out onto the frozen lake. She was right. Gloria could see the corner of the shanty. "And?"

"Well, I was thinking. There are still a couple hours of daylight left. What if you and I kind of took a peek inside the shanty, you know, see if we can find any other clues."

"But how are we going to get inside? I'm sure the police have locked it up tight."

Margaret frowned. "It could present a problem. Is there a way *to* lock the shanty?"

Gloria had no idea. She shrugged. It was worth a try. Still, the thought of making the long trek through Margaret's backyard and across the frozen lake with crutches was less than appealing.

"We can take the snowmobile and be there in no time flat."

Gloria shifted on her crutches. She would love to get a better look inside the shanty.

Margaret could see Gloria was waffling. "We'll take a shovel and I'll clear around it."

Her friend had a well-thought out plan. If Officer Joe Nelson thought the girls were snooping around, this might be their last chance to get close to the scene of the crime.

Gloria sucked in a breath. A little voice whispered in her ear to say "no" as Officer Stan Woszinski's words echoed in the back of her mind...

"Okay. Let's go."

***

Gloria waited on the deck while Margaret headed to the side of the garage to get the snowmobile.

She gazed up at the skies as a nagging feeling in the pit of her stomach told her this might not end well. For the trillionth time, she wished she had never broken her leg and she couldn't wait for the cast to come off.

The roar of a snowmobile engine filled the air and Margaret soon appeared. She eased the snowmobile close to the deck steps, hopped off and handed Gloria a helmet. "You'll need to put this on."

Gloria slipped the helmet on her head and fastened the buckle under her chin. "You do know how to drive this, right?"

Margaret grinned. "Of course. It has been a few years, though," she admitted. She swung her leg over the seat and plopped down before reaching behind her and patting the back seat. "If it's more comfortable, you can sit sideways."

Gloria held onto her crutches as she hopped over to the running machine and backed onto the seat.

Margaret handed her the shovel. "You'll have to hold this."

Gloria grasped the shovel, along with her crutches. She held the three of them with one hand and held onto the safety bar with the other. "I'm ready." *As I'll ever be,* she added silently, wondering how she let her friends talk her into some of the things that they did.

Lucy with her weapons and Ruth with her surveillance equipment were bad enough, but now Margaret?

Maybe the women needed more hobbies to keep them busy. Of course, Lucy's gung-ho gun obsession and Ruth's high tech surveillance equipment collection could both be considered hobbies.

As she rode, Gloria wondered what her hobby was. Sleuthing? That, and gardening, for sure.

Gloria had met the girls for lunch at Dot's Restaurant right after returning from her honeymoon and all had unanimously agreed Belhaven had been boring without her. They couldn't wait for her to come home.

She wondered what in the world they had done before they started all of their investigations. It was hard to remember that far back.

For years, their sleepy little town had been a safe haven. It wasn't until a couple years ago Gloria had started keeping her doors locked. Of course, the world was a lot different place now than it used to be. The criminal element was everywhere!

"We're here," Margaret announced as she came to an abrupt stop in front of Ed Mueller's shanty.

The door to the shanty was wide open and small snowdrifts had started to form around the doorframe and blow inside, filling the corners. Yellow police tape crisscrossed the open door.

Gloria frowned at the accumulating snow and then down at her leg. She had covered her foot and part of her cast with a plastic bread bag to keep it dry and then pulled one of Paul's boots over the top but she was still nervous about getting it wet.

Margaret, noting Gloria's anxious glance, climbed off the snowmobile and reached for the shovel. "I'll shovel a path."

She placed the tip of the shovel on the ice and marched forward as she shoveled a path from the snowmobile to the open shanty door.

Margaret returned moments later and held out a hand. "You want to just lean on me instead of trying to get across the ice on crutches?"

There was only a short distance between the snowmobile and the open door. Gloria nodded.

Margaret leaned forward and slipped her shoulder under Gloria's arm, lifting her forward as Gloria put all her weight on her good leg.

The women shuffled to the shanty and then studied the open door frame. The small wooden door was hanging from one hinge.

Gloria squinted her eyes and studied the frame. Chunks of splintered wood hung from the frame where the lock had been. "Someone busted this door to get inside."

She shifted her gaze. There wasn't much to see inside the shanty. In the far corner was a plastic five-gallon bucket. On one wall of the shanty was a small shelf. On top of the shelf was a black and white portable television.

In another corner was a portable space heater sitting atop another bucket but the bucket wasn't sitting flush on the ice. It tilted at an odd angle.

Gloria glanced at the police tape, covering the door. "I think there's something under the bucket. I wish we could see what it was."

Margaret lifted the shovel. "We could tip it over using this." She didn't wait for Gloria to reply as she slid the shovel across the smooth ice surface so that the tip was under the gap between the bucket and the ice.

She jerked the handle up, flipping the bucket over and causing the space heater to crash onto the ice.

Gloria's eyes widened. "Well, I'll be."

***

Underneath the bucket was a chain saw. "Someone used the chainsaw to cut a hole in the ice and dump Ed Mueller's body into it." Gloria theorized. "Andrea took a few pictures before the police made us leave the other day. As soon as we get back to your place, I'm going to give her a call."

Either the police had already seen the chainsaw and dismissed it as evidence or someone had just put it there. Perhaps whoever had kicked in the door?

She glanced at the back of the Mueller cottage. The snow was coming down harder now. Soon, any tracks leading from the lake to the Mueller property would be covered with snow. "Can you drive us up to the edge of the ice?"

She didn't want to drive onto the property. If investigators returned and noticed fresh snowmobile tracks, they might become suspicious.

Margaret nodded and tucked her shoulder under Gloria's arm as she helped her make her way back to the snowmobile.

Gloria settled onto the back seat as she balanced the shovel and the crutches in one hand.

Margaret revved up the snowmobile's engine, turned the skis and drove toward the shoreline. She stopped near the edge of the lake.

Gloria propped the shovel against the snowmobile and positioned her crutches under each arm as she hobbled over a small pile of fresh snow and onto the back lawn.

There were several sets of shoe and boot prints and they were heading in every direction. Investigators if Gloria had to guess.

Margaret shifted to the left, glanced at the cottage and then back to the lake. "The shanty is straight out from here.

Gloria made her way over to where Margaret was standing. She gazed at the shanty and then at the backside of the cottage. "Someone had to have dragged Mueller's body onto the ice. Either that, or they killed him inside the ice shanty, but that would be kind of hard to do."

She was stumped. The killer's weapon had been an ice pick but there hadn't been any blood, at least not that she had seen. No blood inside the ice shanty. No blood inside the cottage. Which meant someone had killed Ed and brought his body onto the lake, but how?

It was possible the killer had driven a vehicle right up to the shanty, which meant anyone and everyone could be a suspect.

She studied the tracks carefully as she plodded toward the cottage. There were tons of prints. If the investigators had combed the property, their own tracks would cover any evidence!

Along with boot and shoe prints, there were several straight lines in the snow, perfectly spaced. Right next to the lines were smaller prints. The prints started near the back porch door.

Gloria followed them with her eyes. The tracks went all the way to the edge of the property and then disappeared when they reached the ice.

"I wish I had my phone!" Gloria's cell phone was in her purse, which was inside Margaret's house.

"I have mine." Margaret pulled her phone from her jacket pocket and turned it on.

Gloria pointed at the lines. "Can you take a couple pictures of the tracks and then text them to my phone?"

Margaret leaned over and tapped the screen. "Got it. I sent them to you." She looked up at the sky. "We better get going. I think the storm is about to let loose."

Gloria limped back to the snowmobile, brushed the coating of snow off the snowmobile seat and sat. She lowered the snowmobile helmet's face shield and waited for Margaret to climb on.

During the ride back to Margaret's, Gloria mentally sifted through the list of potential killers. Could it be Sally Keane was the killer? What about Officer Joe Nelson? Maybe he was trying to cover up. Or maybe it was Ed's wife, Sheryl.

If Sally was telling the truth and Ed was a womanizer, Sheryl may have made a surprise trip to Belhaven to catch her husband in the act and in a fit of rage, killed him. Motive and opportunity.

Gloria thought about the cop, who had argued with Ed Mueller the night before his body had been found.

He may have been one of the last people to see Ed Mueller alive.

Margaret squeezed the throttle and they sped across the lake. When they reached Margaret's property, she drove across the backyard and around front, coming to a stop next to Gloria's car.

She slid off the sled, unbuckled her helmet and placed it on the seat.

Gloria grinned as she removed her helmet and handed it to Margaret. "Valet parking," she joked.

Margaret took the helmet and the shovel. "I feel bad about dragging you out to the shanty."

She removed her gloves and placed them on top of the helmet. "I'll be right back. I'm going to grab your purse from inside." Gloria had left her purse on Margaret's dining room table before heading out onto the patio.

Margaret returned moments later. "So what do you think?" she asked as she handed Gloria her purse.

"There are a couple things," Gloria said as she unzipped her purse and fumbled around inside searching for her car keys. "First of all, the chain saw.

I still have to have Andrea send me the pictures she took the day we saw Ed Mueller's body submerged in the ice."

She went on. "Second of all, there was no blood."

"Not that we could see," Margaret pointed out. "It could be whoever killed Ed, cleaned up afterward."

True. Surely, investigators had equipment to test for blood residue. Still, even if they had found blood inside the Mueller's cottage or even the shanty, investigators wouldn't divulge that information.

"If Ed Mueller was stabbed with an ice pick, it was a crime of passion, not a premeditated murder." Gloria climbed into her car, shoving the crutches onto the passenger seat. She shut the door, started the car and rolled down the window.

"I'm going to take a look at the pictures Andrea took and the ones you took. Maybe I can start piecing together the events leading up to Ed's death."

Margaret leaned forward. "Let me know if I can help."

Gloria grabbed her seatbelt and shoved the buckle into the latch. "Will do." She shifted the car in reverse and backed out of Margaret's driveway, her mind spinning at the new clues.

Her gut told her the killer was lurking nearby, watching. Maybe it was time to set a trap and plan an old-fashioned stakeout...right after the snowstorm moved out!

Chapter 16

Gloria parked Annabelle in the garage, closing the garage door behind her. She squeezed past the car as she hobbled to the side service door and opened it.

The snow was coming down in full force and it felt as if she had stepped into a virtual snow globe.

The skies had finally let loose and the storm the forecasters had been predicting was finally upon them. She said a small prayer for Paul...and all her friend's safety as she carefully inched her way across the drive and into the house.

Mally was waiting by the door. Gloria stepped in and Mally darted out.

She watched through the window as Mally romped in the fresh snow, and then rolled around a few times before patrolling the perimeter of the yard.

The wooden chair near the kitchen window was the perfect spot to pull off her boots and set them in the tray. Next, she removed the rubber band that was holding the plastic bread bag in place, along with the bag and placed both inside the boot before turning her attention to dinner.

Gloria shifted in her chair and caught a glimpse of Lucy's yellow jeep as it pulled into the drive. She parked off to the side, hopped out of the driver's side and then raced across the yard.

"I wish I could do that," Gloria muttered under her breath.

Lucy's red head appeared in the window of the porch door and Gloria waved her in.

Mally, who had finished her yard inspection, led the way, shaking off her thick coat of snow when she reached the kitchen. The wet snow pelted Gloria, Lucy and even poor Puddles who had made his way into the kitchen.

Lucy plopped down in the seat Gloria had just vacated and wiggled out of her snow boots, placing them in the plastic bin before unbuttoning her winter jacket and hanging it on the hook near the door. "I tried to call and when you didn't answer, I started to worry. I thought maybe you fell on the ice or something."

"I was on my way home from Eleanor's house when Margaret asked me to stop by. Did you hear Ed Mueller was stabbed with an ice pick?"

Lucy wrinkled her nose. "Yeah. What a horrible way to die."

She bounced over to the counter, where Gloria was pulling dishes from the cupboard. "Whatcha making? Can I help?"

"I have an extra container of goulash Dot sent home the other day and I was going to make some homemade dinner rolls and baked potatoes to go with it."

"Sounds delicious," Lucy said. "Do you want some help?"

"Sure." Gloria nodded. "Let's make a deal. I let you help me and then you stay for dinner."

"Sounds good," Lucy agreed.

Now that Paul and Gloria had married, Gloria felt a little guilty she wasn't able to spend as much time with her friends, especially Lucy and Ruth, both of whom lived alone.

Lucy and her boyfriend, Max, were still going strong. Ruth kept a tight lid on her love life but Gloria had driven by her friend's home in recent weeks and noticed Steve Colby's car parked in the drive on the weekends.

Paul and Gloria were still adjusting to married life, having both lived alone for several years, but so far there had only been a couple small misunderstandings and no major blowouts.

"I put a few potatoes in a pail on the basement steps." The door to Gloria's old Michigan basement was in the dining room, right next to the stairs leading to the second floor. Unlike some of the other old farms in the area, hers did not have an access door from the outside, for which Gloria was thankful.

Lucy reappeared moments later, juggling a few potatoes and she headed to the kitchen sink.

Lucy knew her way around Gloria's home like the back of her hand. She reached into Gloria's junk drawer and pulled out a potato scrubber. After she scrubbed the potatoes, she stabbed them with a fork, placed them in the microwave and turned it on.

While Lucy worked on prepping the potatoes, Gloria placed several frozen dinner rolls on top of a baking sheet. She warmed the oven so she could pop the rolls inside for a quick rise and then settled in at the kitchen table.

Lucy slid into the chair across from Gloria and shifted her gaze as she eyed the lemon cake on top of the fridge.

Gloria followed her gaze. "Help yourself."

"Not without coffee." Lucy popped back out of the chair and headed to the coffee pot. She placed a new coffee filter in the brew basket, added some fresh ground coffee and then water in the reservoir before plucking the lemon cake from the top of the fridge and settling back in at the table.

Gloria sighed heavily as Lucy pulled the plastic lid off the cake. "I never knew how much I took being able to get around for granted." She tapped the top of her cast. "I am so tired of this thing," she griped.

"At least it's only temporary." Lucy tried to cheer her up. "Just think, not long after the cast comes off, we get to go on our cruise!"

True. It wouldn't be long before the girls set sail on their much-anticipated cruise vacation. Gloria and

Margaret had sent in the final payment two weeks ago. Now all they had to do was wait.

The only thing that concerned Gloria was her sister, Liz, who had invited herself and her best friend, Frances, to join Gloria and the girls on the cruise.

Her one small consolation was that at least Liz wouldn't be in the same suite, although across the hall from Gloria was still too close.

She pushed the thought of Liz aside. It would all work out in the end, just as it had during Gloria's honeymoon...even though it was on Liz's lot Gloria had fallen into the hole and broken her leg!

"What do you think happened to Ed Mueller?"

Gloria explained her theory of someone killing Ed in a fit of jealous rage. "Think about it. Officer Joe Nelson and Ed were arguing in front of the Quik Stop the night before his body was found. Sally Keane told me Ed was a player and had hit on her."

Lucy tilted her head. "Oh my gosh! You think Officer Nelson killed Ed?"

"I'm not ruling anyone out, including Sally or Ed's wife, Sheryl." Gloria scraped a small speck off the kitchen table with the tip of her fingernail. "That reminds me. I need to have Andrea send me the pictures of the crime scene."

"The coffee is ready." Lucy headed to the counter while Gloria reached for her cell phone to text Andrea.

Andrea quickly replied. "They're on their way. I hope you're at home. I was just out on the roads and they're a sheet of ice."

"I'm not going anywhere," Gloria texted back.

Lucy set a fresh cup of coffee in front of Gloria and slid a wedge of lemon cake next to it. She cut a large piece for herself and grabbed a fork. "Did she send the pictures?"

Gloria squinted at the phone screen. "Yeah, but I can't see anything on this small screen."

Lucy placed a large piece of cake in her mouth. "I'll go get your laptop," she mumbled.

Gloria's children had surprised her with a brand new laptop computer for Christmas, which was much faster than her old one.

Lucy returned with the laptop in hand and placed it between Gloria and her.

"Thanks Lucy. Maybe you should move in until the cast is off so you can help me." She lifted the lid on the computer and sipped her coffee as she waited for it to warm up.

Gloria sifted through her emails. It seemed like every day she was getting more and more spam and every day she had to unsubscribe to something she had absolutely no use for. "How would you like a pepper prepper for your birthday?"

Lucy scrunched her forehead. "A pepper prepper?"

"Never mind." Finally, Gloria made it through her inbox and found both Andrea and Margaret's emails. She clicked on Andrea's first and then tapped on the picture to enlarge it.

Both women leaned in. "What are we looking for?" Lucy asked.

"I'm not sure," Gloria confessed.

She moved to Margaret's email and clicked on the picture to enlarge it. "Those tracks are a clue, but for the life of me, I can't figure out what it is."

Gloria cut a piece of lemon cake and popped it in her mouth. "Margaret and I found a chainsaw underneath a bucket in Ed Mueller's ice shanty."

Lucy's eyes widened. "I thought someone stabbed him with an ice pick, not cut him up into little pieces."

Gloria rolled her eyes. "No, no. The chain saw was for cutting the ice to drop his body in the lake, not cutting him into itty bitty pieces."

Lucy nodded. "Oh...Gotcha! Go on."

After Gloria hashed out the clues and then ticked off the limited list of suspects, she hopped over to the warm oven, popped the dinner rolls inside and turned the oven timer on.

Lucy reached for the lemon cake and deftly sliced off a second piece. "Well, it's probably Sally Keane. Remember we found her nametag in Ed Mueller's trash."

Gloria wasn't convinced it was Sally. Perhaps the killer was trying to set Sally - or even Officer Joe Nelson - up. Perhaps it was Sheryl Mueller. "We need to be one hundred percent certain, which is why we need to set a trap."

"How we gonna do that?"

"I don't know. I haven't gotten that far yet," Gloria said.

Paul pulled in the drive at the same time the timer for the dinner rolls chimed.

Gloria let Lucy pull them from the oven and set them on top of the stove while she grabbed a stick of butter from the refrigerator and made her way to the stove to butter the tops.

Lucy pulled one of the baked potatoes from the microwave and stabbed it with a fork. "Almost done," she said as she slipped it back inside the microwave and turned it back on. "Can I do anything else?"

Gloria nodded over her shoulder. "You can get the goulash from the fridge, put it in a bowl and warm it in the microwave.

Paul opened the kitchen porch door and a blast of cold winter air burst into the room. Gloria shivered.

"Sorry." He stomped his feet on the rug and settled into the chair near the door. "The roads are treacherous." He glanced at Lucy as he removed his boots. "It's a good thing you don't have far to drive."

Lucy's small ranch was less than two miles from Gloria's farm and on the same road leading into the small town of Belhaven.

He wiggled his feet out of his wet boots and set them on the overflowing boot tray. "They said the storm isn't going to let up until after midnight."

"What about driving to work tomorrow?" Gloria fretted. The thought of Paul driving on the snowy country roads with a layer of ice hidden underneath the snow caused her concern.

"They'll have it plowed by the time I leave in the morning," he assured his wife as he made his way over to the stove and snuck a kiss. "How was your day?"

"Same old, same old," Gloria replied as she turned her face toward him.

Lucy snickered.

Paul nodded knowingly. "Uh-huh. How did Margaret's hypnosis experiment turn out?"

"Good grief! What a hot mess!" Gloria grinned. "It ended with Margaret clearing Eleanor's kitchen table so Eleanor could lie down on top of it."

"Then Eleanor fell asleep," Lucy added.

"So it was a bust?"

"Not completely. She finally remembered it was Officer Joe Nelson she had seen down at the Mueller cottage the night before Ed's body was discovered."

Gloria's cell phone, which was sitting on the kitchen table, began to chirp. Gloria hopped to the table and peered at the screen. It was Ruth.

"Hello?"

"I'm still at work. You'll never guess who the cops just put in the back of a patrol car!"

Chapter 17

Gloria had no idea but knew she was about to find out. "Who?"

"Kate Edelson!"

Kate Edelson was Bea McQueen's daughter. Bea was the town's resident hairdresser and a huge gossip to boot.

Kate had moved to Belhaven and in with her mother a couple months back. According to Ruth, the young woman was in the midst of a nasty divorce and custody battle with her soon-to-be-ex.

Gloria had caught glimpses of the pretty, petite brown-haired woman around town but had never officially met her nor even had a conversation, although Ruth knew all about her.

Brian Sellers, Andrea's fiancé, had recently hired her to work part-time at the Quik Stop.

"What happened?"

"Well, Gus's wife, Mary Beth, was just here. She said she'd been in the Quik Stop picking up a couple things for dinner when there was a sudden ruckus back behind the deli counter so she went over to find out what was going on."

"Hang on. Got a customer."

Gloria turned the phone to speaker. "You gotta hear this," she told Paul and Lucy.

They silently listened as Ruth talked to someone in the background. "I'm back. She said the two women were screaming at each other. Next thing Mary Beth knows, Sally throws a punch and lands a hard one to the corner of Kate's jaw and knocks her to the floor."

"Kate grabbed Sally's blouse and pulled her down with her. After that, it was an all-out brawl. Mary Beth didn't know what to do so she called 911 on her cell phone."

Gloria sucked in a breath.

"We need some popcorn," Lucy giggled.

"The cops pulled up in front of the store a few minutes ago and I watched them put Kate in the back of the squad car."

Gloria shook her head. "But why not arrest Sally, too?" It sounded as if Sally had been the one to initiate the physical altercation.

"Because Officer Joe Nelson was the one who showed up."

"That's not right," Lucy said. "They both should've been arrested."

Ruth cut in. "I gotta go. Bea is here."

The line went dead and Gloria set the phone on the edge of the kitchen table. Was Ed having a fling with this woman, too?

He didn't strike Gloria as the kind of man women would fight over...or kill over. Perhaps there had been an entirely different reason the two women had brawled.

Sally was a constant complainer and Gloria was certain there was no way she could work with Sally for any length of time without wanting to strangle her or grab a roll of duct tape and seal her mouth shut.

The trio settled in around the table Lucy had set and then bowed their heads to pray. "Dear Lord, we thank you for this food. We thank you for all of our blessings and all you have given us. Lord, we pray for those traveling on the slippery roads tonight - for our family and friends and for safety. Last, but not least, we pray for Ed Mueller's family. Thank you, Father, most of all, for your Son, our Savior, Jesus Christ."

Gloria was about to say amen when Lucy chimed in. "And that you help us uncover Ed Mueller's killer. Amen."

Lucy lifted her head and reached for the goulash bowl sitting next to her plate. She scooped a large spoonful onto her plate and then passed the bowl to Gloria.

Gloria placed one large scoop on the edge of her plate and then handed the bowl to Paul. She placed a baked potato on her plate and cut it with her fork, spreading the potato out on the center of her plate and flattening it with the tines.

The butter she'd used to butter the rolls had softened and she expertly sliced a pat off and smeared it over the hot potato. "I can't wait to find out what Bea has to say."

Paul reached for a dinner roll. "I hope Joe Nelson wasn't playing favorites."

Gloria broke a piece of her warm roll off, put it in her mouth and chewed thoughtfully. Sally must have a lot of sway over the cop. Was he trying to cover for Sally...or was Sally trying to cover for him? She turned to her husband. "You don't think..."

Paul began shaking his head. "You know this isn't my investigation." He caught the pleading look in his bride's eyes and caved...slightly. "All right. If I hear anything, I'll let you know, but I'm not going to start poking around, asking questions."

Gloria reached over and squeezed his hand. "I knew I could count on you."

The conversation turned to the raging storm. Gloria glanced out the kitchen window. It was a complete whiteout and she couldn't even see Mally's favorite tree near the edge of the driveway. She turned to her friend. "You sure you don't want to spend the night?"

"I can't. Jasper is home."

Gloria had forgotten all about Lucy's dog, Jasper. There was no way Lucy could leave her home alone all night.

"I can follow you home," Paul offered.

"I'll be fine," Lucy reassured them, "but I'll probably hit the road as soon as we finish eating."

Gloria refused to let Lucy help her clean up and instead insisted she head out before the snow drifted on the roads even more.

Lucy slipped her feet inside her boots, then put her coat on and pulled a cap on her head before reaching for her purse and keys.

Paul held the door as Lucy stepped out onto the porch and into the storm, and then disappeared in a swirl of white.

"I hope she makes it home okay." The snow was blinding. Gloria couldn't see Lucy or her vehicle. She caught a glimpse of red from the jeep's taillight, which was quickly swallowed up in the storm.

Gloria stood by the door, cell phone in hand and anxiously stared out at the whirling white snow until Lucy called ten minutes later to let her know she'd arrived home safely.

Paul refused to let Gloria help clean up the dinner dishes. She sat at the kitchen table and watched, feeling helpless as he cleared the table and then washed and dried the dishes.

He had just finished drying the drink glasses and had placed them in the kitchen cupboard when Gloria's house phone rang. It was Ruth.

"You'll never guess what Bea told me!"

***

Gloria covered the mouthpiece of the phone. "It's Ruth," she whispered to Paul as she hobbled into the dining room to talk.

She eagerly turned her attention to the phone conversation. "What did she say?"

Ruth went on to tell her Sally had complained about Kate, which wasn't a surprise. First, she'd complained to Brian that she didn't like Kate, then that Kate was having a hard time catching on and finally that it was taking too long to train her.

Next, she accused Kate of snooping through her personal belongings, which she kept locked in a cabinet in the rear of the store. The last straw had been when Sally accused Kate of stealing her nametag.

Gloria mulled over the new information and spoke her thoughts. "Perhaps Ed and Sally were having a fling and met up at his cottage. When he got home, he remembered Sally had left her nametag at the cottage. Ed, not wanting his wife to find Sally's nametag, made a special trip to Belhaven to get rid of the evidence and had thrown it in the trash," she theorized.

Ruth picked up. "Sally showed up at Ed's cottage after finishing her shift at the store. They got into some sort of argument and in a fit of rage she killed him. When she realized he was dead, she panicked. She dragged his body down to the ice shanty, cut a hole and dropped him in, hoping any evidence on his body would disappear in the icy grave."

It was a possibility, a strong possibility but what about Officer Joe Nelson? Had Sally confessed her crime to him and he was trying to help her cover it up...or had he stumbled upon Sally and Ed arguing in the store, confronted him on the sidewalk, followed him to his cottage and then killed him?

Last, but not least, was Ed's wife, Sheryl. Perhaps she had grown suspicious and driven to Belhaven to confront her husband, found Sally's nametag inside the cottage before Ed had a chance to get rid of it and then killed him in a fit of rage.

"Three suspects, with both motive and opportunity," Ruth said. "Now to figure out how to flush out the killer. What's the plan?"

Gloria gazed out at the snow through the dining room window. Small piles of the white stuff filled the corner of the window frame.

Her first thought was to set a trap, to flush out the killer, but then she had another thought. What if they were somehow able to weasel out a confession?

Gloria had once watched as Joyce Jameson, the character on her favorite detective show, had tricked a killer into confessing by bluffing. "I have a couple thoughts but need to sleep on it."

"Yeah, I need to get home. I can't even see Dot's Restaurant across the street," Ruth said. It was a good thing Ruth's home was in town and only a couple blocks from the post office.

"Call me in the morning," Gloria said before she disconnected the line and headed to the kitchen to put the phone up.

On her way to the phone cradle, she passed by the kitchen counter and spied Alice's "special" spice container sitting on the counter. She picked up the container and held it to the light. It was half-empty!

She carried it to the kitchen doorway and gazed through the dining room into the living room where she could see Paul lounging in his recliner, remote in hand.

Gloria made her way into the living room and held up the container. "Did you try this?"

Paul turned his attention to his wife. "Yeah. I was getting Mally a dog treat and saw it in the back of the pantry. It smelled spicy and I remembered the boys' chips and salsa the other night and it made me want some."

Paul loved spicy foods. "Did Alice make it?"

"She sure did," Gloria said as she closely studied her husband's face for flickers of flaming passion.

"I dumped a bunch in with some salsa I found in the fridge and then ate it with a couple chips."

"How...much did you mix in the salsa?" she asked.

"More than I wanted," he said. "It poured out kinda fast but don't worry. I ate it all."

Gloria wasn't worried. She was terrified. "How are you feeling?"

Paul reached out a hand. "Why don't you come on over here and find out? Hmm?"

He lowered his lids and crooked his finger.

Gloria's eyes grew wide. Had Alice somehow managed to create a homegrown version of the stuff they advertised on television? Vergola...viagran...

"Let...let me put this back in the cupboard." She turned around and slowly shuffled to the kitchen. Surely, it couldn't be as potent as Alice had warned. Would they be up all night? Paul had to work...she had plans for tomorrow...

Gloria plucked a water glass from the cupboard, filled it with ice and then added tap water. She slowly hobbled into the living room, balancing on one crutch.

Paul turned when he heard his wife and jumped out of his recliner. "Here, let me help." He took the glass of water and placed it on the end table situated between their recliners. "You're getting pretty good at balancing on one crutch."

Gloria nodded as she settled into her recliner. She reached down and pulled the lever, lifting the footrest.

Mally jumped on the footrest and crept onto Gloria's lap. Ever since she'd come home from her honeymoon, Mally...and Puddles had been careful to avoid Gloria's broken leg.

Gloria patted Mally's head absentmindedly as she watched the special weather report on the storm. It was a doozy and she was glad she wasn't out in it.

The special weather report ended and the channel returned to the regularly scheduled program – a presidential debate was in progress. Gloria groaned. "Not another one! How many of these debates are there?" It seemed as if there was a debate every other night.

"I have no idea." Paul changed the channel and they started watching a football game.

Gloria closed her eyes and promptly nodded off.

"Ready for bed?" Paul's voice was close...close to her ear.

Gloria and Mally both jumped.

"The game is over," Paul said as he reached over and rubbed her arm.

Gloria glanced at the living room grandfather clock. It was only nine. "Yeah, we can turn in early." She peered out the large picture window. The snow had let up a little, which meant there was hope the county would plow the roads before Paul had to leave in the morning.

She let Mally out for a quick bathroom break while Paul got ready for bed.

The old farmhouse had one inside bathroom. There was another bathroom in one of the outbuildings just off the back porch but Gloria hadn't used it in years.

She gave Puddles and Mally a small snack before heading to the now empty bathroom.

Paul was watching television in bed by the time Gloria made her way in. "They're cancelling schools right and left for tomorrow."

That meant Tyler and Ryan more than likely had a snow day. The buses would have trouble navigating the backroads and many of the side roads would be drifted shut. "The boys will be home tomorrow. Maybe I'll run by Jill's place if the main roads are clear."

Paul waited until Gloria was under the covers before shutting off the television. "Nothing like a little snowstorm to make you want to cuddle."

Paul pulled his wife into his arms and kissed her passionately.

Gloria's toes started to tingle. Perhaps Alice's special love potion wasn't so bad after all...

Chapter 18

Gloria awoke before the alarm sounded the next morning. Although the evening had been wonderful, it had ended up being a restless night. Between the wind howling and rattling the bedroom window, to the thoughts bouncing around in her head on how to either flush out Ed Mueller's killer or trick the killer into confessing, she had tossed and turned for hours.

On the one hand, a good old-fashioned stakeout was exciting, but then she had never tried to coerce a full out confession. Sally would be the perfect candidate to try the latter on. The woman loved to talk...mostly about herself.

Gloria's tentative strategy would be more of "suggesting" something that would cause Sally to panic and confess. She needed to map out the timeline for the events leading up to Ed Mueller's death and tie them to the clues they had thus far. Unfortunately, there weren't many.

Sally's nametag was the biggest clue. She thought about the tracks in the snow. Somehow, someone had been able to move Ed Mueller's body out to the shanty, unless, of course, they had killed him during an argument *inside* the shanty. That would make the most sense.

The inside of the shanty was small. If two people were in the midst of a life and death struggle, wouldn't there be signs the struggle? There was always the possibility the police had already removed all of the evidence.

The shanty door had been busted open. Someone had been desperate to get inside the shanty - perhaps to look for a nametag?

Gloria, deep in her musings, jumped when the alarm sounded. Paul shut the alarm off and threw the covers back before swinging his legs over the side of the bed. "One more day and then the weekend off."

It was time to kick the investigation into high gear. Paul would be home for the weekend and they had already planned to run over to his farm to sort through more things they planned to donate to the Salvation Army in nearby Green Springs.

They had also invited all of the kids – Jill, Greg and the boys, along with Paul's children - his son,

Jeff, daughter-in-law, Tina, and his youngest, Allie, for a late Saturday afternoon dinner.

It would be a busy weekend.

Gloria crawled out of bed and hopped to the window. She lifted the edge of the blind and peered out. It was still dark but she could see the mercury light on the corner of the barn. The snow had stopped.

The newlyweds had already gotten into a small routine, especially when Paul was working. Gloria would let Mally out, then start a pot of coffee and either fix a quick breakfast of scrambled eggs, bacon and a side of toast or go for something quicker and easier – a bowl of cereal and a pastry.

Paul wasn't fussy and Gloria appreciated the fact he never grumbled no matter what was waiting for him on the kitchen table.

She had just started the coffee and made her way over to the fridge when he appeared in the door. "I'm going to shovel the porch and sidewalk before I leave," he said.

Gloria turned. "What about breakfast?"

"I'll hit one of the drive-thru fast food places on my way." He kissed the top of her forehead and walked over to the chair by the door to slip his boots on. "I know there's no way you're going to sit home today and I don't want you struggling to make it across the snow covered porch or sidewalk."

He eased into his coat, zipped the front, pulled on a hat and stepped onto the porch.

Gloria watched as he made quick work of shoveling the porch and a path leading to the garage. "Thank you Lord for such a wonderful husband," she whispered. Her heart warmed as she watched him.

When he came back inside, Gloria had a travel mug filled with fresh, hot coffee waiting for him.

She hugged him, despite his cold, snowy jacket and laid her head against his chest. "Thank you. That was so thoughtful." Her voice cracked and sudden tears burned the back of her eyes.

"You're welcome. Anything to keep my beautiful bride safe."

She lifted her face and Paul gently kissed her lips. "You can pay me back later," he flirted.

Gloria's stomach fluttered and her eyes grew wide. Was Alice's "Love Potion" still working its magic?

Mally slipped in when Paul made his way out. He had also brushed the snow off his truck and started the engine. She waved from the doorway, unsure if he could even see her.

When his truck disappeared onto the main road, she closed the door and looked down at her beloved pooch. "I better get ready. We have a lot to do today."

Gloria grabbed her crutches and hobbled to the bathroom. She peeled off her pajamas, plugged the bathtub drain and turned on the hot water.

The steamy bath warmed her bones and twice she added more hot water. She stayed in the tub until Mally began whining at the door.

"Okay. I'll get out."

Getting out of the tub was trickier than getting in. It was a balancing act since she had to be careful to keep her cast from getting wet.

Once she was out, she towel dried her body and went over the day's schedule in her mind.

First, she was going to call Jill to see if she and the boys were going to be home. After that, she was going to stop at the post office to find out if Ruth had heard anything else.

Gloria's stomach grumbled and she added a stop at Dot's Restaurant for breakfast to her to-do list. Not only would she be able to bounce some ideas off her friend, she would enjoy a home-cooked breakfast while she was at it.

Rounding out her list was something she had vowed to do for a long time now, which was pay a visit to At Your Service.

She spent extra time in the bathroom making sure her hair was completely dry before applying some makeup and then dressing.

She pulled on a pair of black sweatpants and a cream-colored sweater. Sweat pants were Gloria's new best friend ever since she discovered she was not able to fit the cast into regular pants. The sweatpants were roomy enough to do the trick. Sweatpants were comfortable and, in her opinion, highly underrated.

Mally was patiently waiting by the bathroom door when Gloria emerged. "What? You want to be my sidekick today? We're going to see if Ryan and Tyler are home. Would you like to see Ryan and Tyler?"

Mally whined, which Gloria took as a yes, and the two of them slowly made their way into the kitchen. She studied the linoleum floor, looking for telltale puddles of water, which were treacherous for her and her crutches.

She grabbed the mop propped up against the wall and swiped at a couple of small puddles near the porch door.

There was still half a pot of coffee in the carafe and she had just poured a cup when the house phone rang. "That's right. I need to call Jill," she reminded herself aloud.

"Hello?"

"Hi Gloria. It's Andrea."

"Hi dear. How are you?"

Andrea sighed heavily. "I'm bored. I think I have cabin fever."

Gloria grinned. "Cabin fever in your big old house?" If Gloria lived in Andrea's magnificent mini-mansion, she would never get bored. In fact, she would light a fire in the library's fireplace and curl up in one of her comfy wingback chairs with a good mystery, although not today.

The day would be jam packed with places to go and people to see. "You can tag along with me today. I have a bunch of errands to run."

"I thought you'd never ask," Andrea said. "When are you leaving?"

Gloria glanced at her worn Bible sitting on the corner cabinet. "I'm going to have a cup of coffee, read my Bible and then head out. Maybe half an hour or so."

"I'll be there with bells on," Andrea said. "Thanks for letting me come along!"

"Don't you want to know where we're going?" Gloria asked.

"Nope. I'm sure whatever you have planned will be exciting," her young friend said before hanging up the phone.

Gloria replaced the phone on the receiver and shuffled to the chair.

Puddles climbed onto her lap, which was his morning ritual for Bible reading, and began purring while Gloria opened her Bible.

"Every good gift and every perfect gift is from above, and cometh down from the Father of lights, with whom is no variableness, neither shadow of turning." James 1:17 (KJV)

Gloria lifted her gaze and stared out the kitchen window. Her life was full of blessings...her children and grandchildren, Paul and her dear friends. She thanked the Lord every day for all He had given her.

She felt guilty over her mumbling and grumbling about her broken leg. Yes, she had broken her leg, but God had provided – Paul who made sure the porch and sidewalk were shoveled so she wouldn't slip and fall. She also had her friends, who called to check on her if they hadn't heard from her.

Gloria smiled as she thought of her family...her grandsons who had made their own breakfasts and fed Gloria's beloved pets so she wouldn't have to.

The thought of all she'd been blessed with caused Gloria to tear up for a second time that day. A tear trickled down her cheek. It wasn't a tear of sadness but a tear of thankfulness for all she had.

She swiped the tear with the back of her hand. Puddles nudged her hand and rubbed his wet nose on Gloria's thumb.

Gloria scratched Puddles' ear as she also thanked God for her beloved pets. With a heart full of gratitude, Gloria closed her Bible and set it back on the corner shelf.

"That's right. I have to call Jill," she reminded herself as she hopped to the kitchen counter and reached for the house phone to call her daughter.

Jill picked up on the first ring and Gloria could hear her grandsons hollering in the background. "Are the natives restless already?"

Jill groaned. "Good heavens. You would think it was Christmas morning. So far, I've broken up two fights, stopped them from setting the living room rug on fire and cleaned up three sinks overflowing with dirty dishes, all before eight a.m."

Gloria smiled. "It looks like the main roads are clear. Andrea, Mally and I are heading out to run some errands and thought we'd stop by for a visit."

"Great! The boys would love to see you, Mom."

"Grams! You're coming to see us?" Tyler must have overheard the conversation and taken the phone from his mother.

"Yes, but not for too long. It will be Andrea, Mally and me."

"Did you find out anything on the coins we found in the barn?" he asked breathlessly.

Gloria frowned. She hadn't even had time to think about the coins, let alone clean them up for a closer inspection. "Not yet. I promise to do it this week. Unless you would like me to bring them to you. You and Ryan can do some research." It was a brilliant idea and one that would keep the boys busy, at least for a couple of minutes.

"Okay! We'll be waiting."

He turned the phone back over to his mother. "What time do you think you'll be here?" her daughter asked.

Gloria glanced at the clock. It was nine. She wanted to stop at the post office, then Dot's for breakfast. It would be late morning. "Probably around eleven thirty? I can stop by a fast food drive-thru and grab some burgers and fries."

"Burgers and fries sound good," Jill said.

"Burgers and fries, burgers and fries," echoed in the background.

A movement caught Gloria's eye and she gazed through the kitchen door. It was Andrea's truck pulling in the drive.

The driver's side door popped open and her young friend hopped out of the truck, her blonde ponytail swinging back and forth as she slammed the door shut and darted across the snowy drive.

"Andrea is here. I'll see you soon." Gloria hung up the phone and shuffled to the door.

Andrea bounded up the porch steps and stomped her feet as Gloria opened the kitchen door. "Well, look at this lovely ray of sunshine." She hugged Andrea, hopped to the side and motioned her in.

The young woman looked adorable in her sunny yellow ski jacket, matching yellow and pink headband and pink moon boots.

"I need to tag along with you when you shop. I love your style."

"Thanks." Andrea grinned, the dimple in her cheek deepening. She rubbed her hands together. "I can't wait to hang out with you today."

Andrea's enormous diamond engagement ring sparkled in the kitchen light. Brian had proposed to Andrea while Paul and Gloria had been honeymooning in Florida.

Gloria rattled off the schedule and Andrea nodded. "Sounds good. You want me to drive?" her young friend offered.

"Well...I was going to take Mally along."

Mally heard her name and trotted over.

"No problem. Brutus rides in the truck all the time."

"That would be wonderful." Riding around on snowy roads in Andrea's four-wheel drive pick-up would be much safer than Gloria's car.

"Let me grab my purse." She disappeared into the back and returned moments later, purse in hand. "Let's get this show on the road!"

Chapter 19

Downtown Belhaven was a beehive of activity and Gloria never would have guessed the large number of residents who were out and about. Perhaps they were like Andrea, suffering from cabin fever and anxious for the arrival of spring.

Winter was wearing on Gloria, as well. She was lucky to have had a brief respite in Florida and had thoroughly enjoyed the sunshine and balmy temperatures.

Andrea veered into the post office parking lot and parked in an open spot on the end.

Gloria waited for Mally to hop out first before sliding out of her seat. The three of them made their way inside.

Ruth was behind the counter, waiting on a customer. She shot Gloria a glance – a look that said she had heard something else. The women stood off to the side to wait.

After the customer left the counter, he dropped his stamped envelopes in the out of town mail slot and exited the post office.

Ruth reached into the top drawer, pulled out her container of dog treats and stepped out into the lobby. "Hey Mally. How're you today?" She patted her head as she gave her the doggie treat.

Mally licked Ruth's hand, chomped down on the treat and headed to the corner to eat it.

They were alone inside the post office except for Kenny Webber, Ruth's right hand man and rural route carrier. He waved at Gloria and continued sorting the mail in the back.

"Kate stopped by here first thing this morning. She's madder than a wet hornet and was on her way to confront Brian Sellers over at Nails and Knobs."

Ruth shook her head. "She said she's going to give him an ultimatum. He either get rid of Sally Keane or she was going to quit."

"It won't end well," Gloria predicted. Although Sally was a pain in the rear, he couldn't fire her just because Kate wanted him to.

Sally would be the type of person to file a lawsuit and Brian, a former circuit court judge, would know she might have a legitimate claim. If anything, the ultimatum would backfire and Kate would end up quitting.

Gloria admired the woman's spunk and she would love to talk to her. There was a good chance the woman had overheard something that would be useful in the investigation.

"Brian is level-headed. He'll calm her down," Gloria said. She turned to Andrea. "We should stop by the hardware store and chat with him after we have breakfast at Dot's."

"You want us to bring you back anything to eat?" Andrea asked Ruth. She felt bad knowing Ruth had to work while Gloria and she were able to enjoy a leisurely breakfast.

Ruth shook her head. "Nah. Thanks for asking. Kenny here." She pointed at Kenny. "Brought in some donuts and gourmet vanilla coffee." She pronounced it "gor-met."

"You're a good man," Gloria hollered out as she hopped to the door and the trio made their way outside.

They crossed the street and Gloria was careful to keep her injured leg high off the ground lest some of the salty, wet road splashed her cast. She hopped onto the sidewalk and lowered her leg.

The restaurant was abuzz with excited chatter. The aroma of freshly brewed coffee greeted them at the door.

Gloria glanced around, finally spying a table for two near the back. The girls reached the table at the same time Dot made her way over with a pot of coffee. Mally crawled under the table in search of scraps of food.

"Well, lookie what the cat dragged in. What are you two up to today?" Dot filled a cup of coffee and set it in front of Gloria.

"Oh, this and that," she said vaguely.

"Did you hear about the knockdown, drag out brawl over at the Quik Stop last night?" Dot tsk-tsked. "Sally better watch it or one day someone is going to clean her clock."

Dot set the pot on the edge of the table and pushed a stray strand of hair back. Gloria looked up at her friend...really looked at her. She looked tired. "Are you okay Dot?"

Dot smiled briefly. "Yeah. I didn't sleep well last night. My bones ached this morning, probably from the cold. I'm just tired...tired of winter, I reckon."

Andrea lifted her coffee cup to her lips and sipped. "Maybe you should think about slowing down, taking more time off."

"I've been thinking about it." Dot nodded her head toward Ray, who was behind the cash register. "We have some friends from years back we've been talking to. They're both a few years younger than Ray and I and they're considering moving to Michigan. They claim they are sick of the heat in the south. It's Rose and Johnnie Morris."

"They'll be moving to the right place," Gloria joked.

Dot went on. "We were thinking about partnering up, selling half the business and splitting the workload."

Dot had mentioned her dear friend, Rose, many times. They had met years ago when Dot and Ray had moved to South Georgia years ago to help care for Ray's uncle during an extended illness. After Ray's uncle died, Dot and Ray had moved back to Belhaven, but Rose and Dot had stayed in touch.

"They should come for a visit first," Gloria suggested.

Dot nodded. "They're coming up next week to have a look around. Now that all of their children are grown and have moved away, they're feeling a little restless and looking for something to keep them busy."

"This place will sure do that!" Andrea said.

"If they decide it's something they want to take on, I'm hoping they get settled before our cruise in early March."

Gloria had wondered how Ray would hold down the fort while Dot was on their cruise vacation. She hoped it would work out and that Ray and Dot could start taking more time off and enjoying a semi-retirement. "I'll pray about it," she simply said.

The customers at the table next to Gloria and Andrea departed, leaving a tower of dirty dishes. "I best get back to work."

Gloria watched as Dot returned the coffee carafe to the burner and made her way over to the dirty table with a bussing bin. She quickly loaded the dirty plates, silverware, cups and glasses.

Dot had finished her cancer treatments not long ago and the girls had celebrated with an afternoon movie matinee and late lunch. They were all thankful that so far, Dot's prognosis was good.

It was time for them...all of them...to slow down and enjoy the golden years. Gloria thought back to the last few years that her first husband, James, had been alive.

They had done a little traveling with a road trip down the East Coast, starting in Maine and ending in the Carolinas. Their last big adventure had been when they circled the Great Lakes in an RV, which reminded Gloria of her recent honeymoon.

Life was too precious to take for granted. A Bible verse popped into Gloria's head:

"Do not boast about tomorrow, for you do not know what a day may bring." Proverbs 27:1 NIV

Ray stopped by a short time later to take their breakfast order. Gloria didn't bother looking at the menu since she knew everything listed by heart. "I'll take an English muffin, scrambled eggs, an order of bacon and it would be great if you could throw a slice of cheddar cheese on the side."

Andrea promptly closed her menu and slid it back in the holder. "Make that two, plus a glass of orange juice."

Ray jotted their order on a pad and then slid it in his front pocket. "Got it."

"Dot tells me your friends, Rose and Johnnie, will be here next week and they're thinking of partnering up and sharing the workload around here."

Ray smiled. "Yeah." He glanced over his shoulder at Dot, who was clearing another table. "It's time to slow down and enjoy life."

He sucked in a breath and shook his head. "I'm worried about Dot. She's trying to do too much and it's wearing her down. It's almost as if the cancer knocked the wind out of her and she hasn't completely recovered yet."

Gloria cradled her coffee cup and studied Ray's face. "I think it's high time you both start taking time off. I can't wait to meet your friends."

Ray grinned. "Whew! They're a couple of characters."

Gloria watched as Ray walked away. Whenever Dot mentioned Rose and Johnnie, she would smile from ear to ear and say they had more personality than anyone she'd ever met.

After the girls finished breakfast, Andrea carried their dirty dishes to the back to save Dot and Ray from having to clean up after them. Andrea also insisted on buying Gloria's breakfast.

She paid for breakfast and returned to the table. "Ready to stop by the hardware store?"

Gloria, so caught up in worrying about Dot and Ray, had completely forgotten. She couldn't wait to find out what had happened after Kate Edelson stormed into Brian's hardware store demanding he fire Sally Keane. She would've loved to have been a fly on the wall, listening in on that conversation.

Andrea held the door and Gloria stepped onto the sidewalk. The sidewalk had been freshly salted and Gloria's crutches crunched under the small pellets of salt.

Andrea held Mally's leash while they walked.

Nails and Knobs was on the same side of the street as Dot's Restaurant, but at the other end.

The sun was trying to peek out from under the thinning clouds and it looked as if it was going to be a beautiful winter day.

When they reached the front entrance to the hardware store, Andrea went first and waited while her friend navigated the three steps.

Once inside, she shoved a crutch under each arm and hustled to the back of the store. Gloria caught Brian's eye and he winked as he rang up a snow shovel for a customer.

After the customer left the store, Gloria turned her attention to the handsome young man behind the counter. "Well?"

Brian lifted a brow and grinned. "Well what?"

"You know what," Andrea squeezed his arm. "How did it go with Kate this morning?"

Brian rested his arms on the counter. "Has Ruth set up some sort of surveillance equipment in here that I don't know about?" he joked.

It was a thought. Honestly, Gloria wouldn't put it past her friend... "Kate stopped by the post office before she came here."

"I calmed her down, explained that Sally was under duress and acting a little irrationally," he said.

Gloria wondered what kind of "duress" Sally was suffering from, but kept quiet.

"Irrationally?" Andrea gasped. "She punched Kate and the two proceeded to brawl on the store floor."

"True, but I can't just up and fire Sally." Obviously, Brian wasn't as alarmed by the incident as they were. Still, having the two women work together wasn't a good idea, at least it wasn't to Gloria.

He went on. "Kate and I went down to the store to meet with Sally. The two women called a truce. I don't think there will be another issue."

Gloria hoped not, for his sake. "Is Kate working now?"

Brian shook his head. "She's working the afternoon shift." He lifted his gaze and stared at the ceiling. "From four to close, if I remember correctly." Brian leveled his gaze on Gloria. "Let me guess. You're going to stop by the store later today."

"Bingo!" Gloria snapped her fingers. That was her exact plan and the sooner the better. She hoped Kate had overheard something that might be useful in moving the murder investigation forward.

Brian walked them to the door. When they reached the entrance, Andrea spun around and stepped into Brian's arms. He pulled her close and gently kissed her lips. "See you later tonight?" he murmured.

Gloria shifted to the side, pretending to study a bag of ice melt. For some reason, the ice melt reminded her that Paul's birthday was right around the corner and she hadn't decided on a gift yet. He didn't need anything, although his fishing gear was in rough shape. Perhaps she could surprise him with a new set.

Andrea pulled away from Brian, her eyes bright and cheeks flushed. "We better get going."

"Paul's birthday is right around the corner. Do you have any fishing gear you can recommend?"

Brian nodded. "You're in luck. I've got a new vendor bringing me some stuff next Tuesday. Stop by late next week and I'll have a ton of equipment for you to choose from."

"As long as you can help me pick it out," Gloria said. "I haven't a clue what to look for in fishing gear."

Brian gave Gloria a quick hug before the girls and Mally stepped back out onto the sidewalk and slowly walked back to the post office parking lot.

Gloria opened the passenger door of the truck and shoved her crutches inside. She grasped the side handle with one hand and the edge of the leather seat with the other.

Climbing into Andrea's pick-up was easier than crawling into Annabelle, at least it seemed that way to Gloria.

Mally jumped into the truck and wiggled her way to the back seat.

Andrea pulled the driver's side door shut and turned to Gloria. "Where to?"

"Jill's place. Start heading toward Rapid Creek and I'll tell you where to turn off."

The drive to Jill's went by quickly as the girls discussed Andrea and Brian's recent engagement, the murder investigation and At Your Service dog training center. They also discussed Dot's health, which was weighing heavily on Gloria's mind.

"I almost feel guilty eating at Dot's," Gloria admitted.

"Me too," Andrea agreed. "If we all stayed away because we didn't want to be a burden to her, then they wouldn't have a business and would have to close the doors."

Gloria tugged on her seatbelt absentmindedly. "The sooner Rose and her husband get here, the better. We need to start praying for a small miracle."

They stopped by a local burger joint in Rapid Creek before heading to Jill's home where Andrea pulled up in front of the house and parked in the street.

Ryan and Tyler exploded out the front door and reached their beloved Grams at the same time she hit the ground, almost knocking her over. "Easy boys! Don't mow her down!" Jill stood on the front porch shaking her head.

Gloria handed each of the boys a bag of food and then Andrea and Gloria followed the boys onto the porch and in through the front door.

Jill had done a magnificent job of decorating their new home. The living room boasted several pieces of new furniture including two overstuffed chairs that faced the cozy fireplace. "The house looks wonderful Jill."

"Thanks Mom. It has been so much fun decorating and adding new furniture. How we ever survived all those years in our tiny bungalow is beyond me."

Ryan and Tyler set the bags of food on the dining room table.

Ryan tugged on Gloria's arm. "Can we take Mally out into the backyard?"

"Of course, but before I forget, I want to give you boys those coins so you can clean them up and then do a little research." She reached inside her pocket and pulled out the coins, dropping a couple into each of their outstretched hands.

Tyler and Ryan placed them on the edge of the kitchen counter and then raced out the back door with Mally in hot pursuit.

"Have a seat." Jill pulled out a chair. "Would you like me to make a pot of coffee?"

"No thanks, unless Andrea wants something."

Andrea shook her head. "I already feel like I'm going to float away. I would love to take a tour of your house though."

Gloria waited near the slider while Jill gave Andrea a grand tour of their home. She watched as the boys chased Mally around in the snow.

The sun was shining brightly and it was almost blinding. Gloria blinked rapidly and then shifted her gaze to the side of the garage where she spotted two plastic sleds propped up against the wall.

The sight of the sleds caused Gloria to have a sudden thought. She unlocked the slider and stuck her head out. "Hey boys. Why don't you take Mally for a ride?" She pointed at the sleds.

Ryan and Tyler raced each other to the sleds and then fought over who would give Mally a ride first. "Why don't you take turns giving Mally and one of you a ride?" she suggested.

Ryan and Mally climbed into the sled while Tyler reached for the plastic yellow rope on the front. She stepped out onto the back deck to watch.

"Riding in the sled looks like fun," she told them when they passed by.

Tyler stopped abruptly and eyed his grandmother. "You want to go for a ride Grams?"

"No. I'll pass, but thanks for asking." She continued to watch as the sled zigzagged back and forth across the yard.

"Time for lunch," Jill called from the doorway.

The boys pulled the sled and Mally to the edge of the deck and then darted up the steps.

Gloria hopped onto the bottom step and leaned forward to stare at the tracks the sled had made. The tracks were eerily similar to the tracks Gloria had noticed in the back of Ed Mueller's yard!

Chapter 20

Gloria hopped to the slider door and stuck her head inside. "Andrea, can you hand me my purse?"

Andrea grabbed Gloria's purse off the counter and brought it to her.

Gloria reached inside, pulled out her cell phone, turned it on and opened her messages. When she got to the one Margaret had sent her, she opened the message and tapped the screen to enlarge the picture.

She squinted at the screen. "I need my reading glasses." She reached inside her purse, opened her glasses case and slipped the glasses on, peering at the screen. "Those tracks are similar to the tracks the boys' sled just made."

Gloria handed the phone to Andrea who gazed at the picture on the screen. She carried the phone to the edge of the deck and stared down at the pattern in the snow. "You're right. What possible reason could Ed Mueller have for dragging a child's plastic sled through the snow?"

"Unless it wasn't Ed Mueller at all, but rather the killer who placed his body inside the sled and then dragged it out onto the ice."

Andrea quickly snapped several pictures of the tracks in the snow before reaching down and tipping the sled upside down. She snapped a couple more pictures of the bottom of one of the sleds and then wandered up the steps.

"Thanks Andrea." Gloria slipped the phone inside her purse. "Finally, the pieces are all starting to fall into place. All we have to do is figure out who killed Ed Mueller!"

***

The boys gobbled their burgers and fries and then ran back outside to play with Mally while the women chatted at the table.

The conversation turned to the dog-training center.

"That reminds me." Andrea glanced at her watch. "We should get going if we want to stop by At Your Service on the way home."

Ryan and Tyler were sad to see Gloria and Mally leave, but their grandmother promised they could come spend the night at the farm soon, which seemed to cheer them up.

The visit to At Your Service was long overdue and Gloria was glad they had carved time into their schedule to stop.

Alice, who was the first to notice them, met them at the door. She hugged Gloria and then pulled away. "You try my love potion on Mr. Paul?"

Gloria grinned and rolled her eyes. "He found it in the pantry last night and mixed half the container with a dish of salsa."

Alice lifted a hand to her lips. Her eyes grew wide. "Oh no. Wh-what happened?"

Alice's face reddened as she realized what she had asked. She waved her hand. "Forget I ask Miss Gloria!"

Andrea groaned and shook her head. "Oh Alice!"

They turned their attention to the dogs and watched as the female trainer taught a young Labrador retriever to respond to commands. The trainer explained the dog needed to be able to respond to the clicker and the best way to do that was associate treats with clicks.

It was fascinating to watch the energetic, adorable and extremely intelligent dog. Gloria would have loved to take him home.

As the trio toured the facility, she was impressed with the cleanliness and organization of the operation. Alice and Mario Acosta had done a fantastic job of turning the former puppy mill into not only a lucrative business but also a facility that would help others.

For the second time, Gloria caught a spark between Mario Acosta and Alice. She wondered how long it would be before the two of them realized it. Andrea might not have a roommate forever!

After the tour ended, Mario promised to bring Alice home later and the women climbed into the truck where Mally patiently waited inside.

Andrea steered the truck out of the drive and headed back toward Belhaven. "Do you still want to stop by the Quik Stop?"

Gloria glanced at the dashboard clock. Kate would be working and Sally Keane gone for the day, unless of course, the two of them had had another brawl and were in jail. "Yeah. If you don't mind."

"Not at all."

When they reached Belhaven, Andrea pulled the truck into an empty spot directly in front of the store and the girls climbed out.

"You wait here," Gloria told Mally. "We'll be right back and I'll bring you a treat."

Gloria wasn't in the mood to make a big meal and decided on frozen pizza for dinner.

She let Andrea carry the shopping basket as the women walked the aisles picking up a few items, including Mally's favorite dog treats.

Gloria caught a glimpse of auburn hair and a petite figure behind the deli counter. The woman finally looked up and Gloria smiled. "Hello. You must be Kate."

She nodded and stepped out from behind the counter. "Yes, and you must be Gloria Kennedy," she replied.

"How did you…"

"The crutches are a dead giveaway," she smiled. "Do you need anything from the deli?"

"No thanks." Gloria turned to Andrea.

Andrea nodded. "I'll take a small container of chicken salad and a pound of shaved ham."

While Kate prepared the order, Andrea and Gloria finished perusing the aisles. They reached the checkout counter at the same time Kate arrived with Andrea's deli items.

She placed them on the counter and Gloria stepped to the side while Andrea paid.

"I heard you and Sally Keane had it out yesterday," Gloria said.

Kate gave Gloria a quick glance and then returned to the task at hand. "Sally is a trip."

"Yes, she can be," Gloria agreed.

Kate rolled her eyes. "Something about me chasing after 'her men.' Like I would want those old farts. A donut eating cop and some slimeball who hits on all the women." She shivered. "The guy gave me the creeps. I have no idea what she saw in him, or what the other woman saw in him, for that matter."

"What other woman?" Andrea and Gloria asked in unison.

"I don't know her name. She was skinny with gray hair." Kate waved her hand dismissively. "I've only seen her once and the only reason I remember is Sally and she were having some sort of heated argument back near produce. I overheard them mention a man's name and only later put two and two together that he was the guy they found in the lake." She shrugged her shoulders.

Gloria shifted on her crutches. "Did you tell that to the police?"

"Yep." Kate nodded. "I guess that was one of the reasons Officer Joe Nelson took me to the station, to ask me about the other woman."

Andrea leaned in. "Did the officer happen to mention the name of the other woman?"

"Yeah, but for the life of me, I can't remember what it was."

"That'll be twelve dollars and eighty nine cents," she told Andrea, who pulled her debit card from her wallet and handed it to the attractive woman.

The wheels in Gloria's head were spinning. Motive – jealousy. Opportunity – what better place than right next door to the victim. "I think I know who killed Ed Mueller."

After Gloria paid for her purchases, the women made their way out of the store and onto the sidewalk. "I'm sure I know who killed Ed Mueller. Now all we have to do is figure out how to get a confession."

"If the police haven't already done it," Andrea pointed out.

Back at the farm, Gloria opened the passenger door and Mally scrambled out. "Thanks for driving today," she told Andrea as she balanced on one leg and reached for the crutches.

"Thank you for letting me tag along," Andrea grinned. The smile quickly faded. "You're not going to try to confront the suspect on your own, are you?"

Gloria shook her head. "No. I have a couple phone calls to make before I do anything." The first call would be to Eleanor Whittaker to ask her if she'd noticed any lights on at the cottage next door to the Mueller's cottage.

She grabbed her groceries, hobbled to the house and up the steps, and then waved to Andrea when she reached the porch.

Mally, who had been patrolling the property, met her at the door.

She shut the door when they were both safely inside.

Gloria dropped her purse on the chair and hung her keys on the hook by the door, along with her jacket. She put her groceries away and a blast of cold air from the fridge caused her to shiver.

The inside of the drafty old farmhouse was chilly so she turned the thermostat up a couple degrees before grabbing her cell phone from her purse and making her way into the dining room.

Before Paul had moved in, Gloria had done some rearranging and her computer desk, which had previously faced the corner, now faced the kitchen. She swung around, took one big hop and plopped down in the chair.

"Drat! I forgot my reading glasses." She switched the phone on and then squinted at the screen as she scrolled through the list of names. When she reached Eleanor's name, she pressed the call button and placed the phone next to her ear.

The phone rang and rang, and Gloria was about to give up when a breathless Eleanor answered. "Hello?"

"Eleanor, it's Gloria. Is everything alright?"

"Yes, I was just putting a fresh batch of cookies on a plate for company and thought I heard the phone ring. It took me awhile to get to it."

"I'm sorry. I didn't mean to make you rush." The thought of Eleanor hurting herself trying to reach the phone caused Gloria to feel guilty for even bothering the poor woman.

"Have you cracked the case?" Eleanor asked anxiously.

"Well, that's why I'm calling. Do you recall seeing any other lights on at the cottages down by the lake…say for example, the cottage to the left of the Mueller's place?"

Silence. Gloria wondered if they'd lost connection. "Hello? Eleanor, are you there?"

"I'm here Gloria. Funny you should say that because I remember a light on in the cottage next door. It was the Clemson cottage."

Gloria's hunch had been correct and she remembered running into Lynda Clemson in the Quik Stop. Lynda fought with Sally over Ed Mueller. Could it be that Lynda confronted Ed Mueller in a fit of rage, they had fought and she killed him?

Eleanor pulled Gloria from her musings. "Oh. Lynda Clemson called a short time ago and asked if she could stop by. That's why I was making cookies. I see her walking through my backyard now. Odd though, that she didn't just drive over. I don't see her car at her place, either. Maybe it broke down."

Gloria tightened her grip on the phone. The woman had been hiding her car in the garage and it was still there because she didn't want anyone to see her car parked in Eleanor's drive!

She interrupted Eleanor. "Eleanor! Whatever you do, don't answer the door. I have a hunch Lynda is the killer. If she thinks you're a witness and may have seen something, your life is in danger!"

"Oh dear!"

Gloria jumped out of her chair and headed to the kitchen to grab the house phone. "Stay on the line, Eleanor. I'm going to use my house phone to call 911!"

Her stomach churned as she hopped on one leg to the kitchen phone. She grabbed the phone, punched in 911 and hit call.

"911. What is your emergency?"

"Someone is trying to break into my friend's house. She lives at 212 Overlook Street, Belhaven, Michigan. We need police there as soon as possible."

"What is your friend's name?"

"Eleanor Whittaker. Please hurry!" Gloria's mouth grew dry, as if she had swallowed a box of cotton balls. She would never forgive herself if anything happened to the sweet lady!

"I have her on the other line."

"Is she able to hang up and call 911 so we can stay on the line with her?" the operator asked.

Gloria talked into her cell phone. "Eleanor. What's happening?"

"She's ringing the front doorbell," Eleanor whispered into the phone.

"Police are on the way. Are you able to hang up and dial 911?"

"Yes. I can do that." The line disconnected.

Gloria talked into the landline. "She just hung up and is going to call."

Gloria disconnected both lines and began praying. "Dear God, please protect Eleanor!"

Gloria was torn. On the one hand, she wanted to hop in the car and race over to Eleanor's. On the other, she didn't want to get in the way. She paced the floor and watched the clock. Five minutes. Ten minutes.

When half an hour passed, her growing concern over Eleanor's welfare won out. She lifted her purse off the chair, slipped her barn Croc on her foot and pulled her jacket on.

As quickly, yet as carefully as possible, she trekked across the yard and into the garage. While the garage door opened, she slid behind the wheel.

She backed out of the driveway and pulled onto the main road. Gloria's cell phone beeped and she glanced at the front. It was Lucy's cell phone.

"Hello?"

"Something is going on over at Eleanor's place! Her drive and street are swarming with cop cars!"

Gloria's breath caught in her throat. "I-Is there an ambulance?"

"Yep," Lucy confirmed. "I'm parked at the end of her street." Lucy relayed the scene. "The police are out of their cars but kind of ducking behind the doors like they do on television during a hostage situation."

Chapter 21

Eleanor Whittaker kept one eye on the shadowy figure outside her front door. Her hand trembled as she dialed 911. "This is Eleanor Whittaker, 212 Overlook Street, Belhaven, Michigan. I think someone is trying to break into my house."

"One moment...yes. We dispatched an officer. He is only a couple minutes away. Can you escape through a back door or barricade yourself in a room until police arrive?"

Eleanor's eyes darted to the living room. "Not without having to walk right by the front door." She gazed at her rear slider. The slider led out onto Eleanor's second floor deck. There were no steps to ground level. If she took that route, she would have to jump.

Eleanor shifted her gaze back toward the living room and the front of the house. On the other side of the living room was a hall leading to the bedrooms. If she could make it past the living room, she could lock herself in her bedroom. "I might have a shot at making it to my bedroom."

Lynda Clemson began pounding on the front door. "Eleanor! Open the door!"

Eleanor dropped onto her hands and knees, the house phone gripped in one hand as she crawled across the floor as quickly as possible in a desperate attempt to reach the hallway.

The front doorknob rattled. Eleanor could tell from the tone of the woman's voice that Lynda Clemson was growing desperate. "I'm going to break in!" she yelled.

Eleanor picked up the pace and scooted across the floor, the skin on her knees rubbing roughly on the orange shag carpet.

Whack! The whole door shook.

Eleanor lifted the phone. "She's kicking the front door open!"

Whack! After the whack came a cracking noise.

Boom! The door flew open and a wild-eyed, crazy-haired Lynda Clemson rushed in.

Lynda's gaze focused on Eleanor...and the phone she had pressed to her ear.

"Give me the phone!" Lynda lunged for the phone, easily ripping it from Eleanor's grip.

She pressed the off button and then hurled the phone across the room before stomping over to the front door and slamming it shut. The busted door swung back open.

Lynda Clemson dragged a nearby chair to the door and shoved it against it to keep it closed before turning to face Eleanor.

"You! It's your fault the police are onto me," she snarled as she waved a gun Eleanor hadn't noticed...probably because the crazed woman was ripping through her house like a banshee.

Lynda reached down, grabbed Eleanor's upper arm and yanked her to her feet, knocking the wind out of poor Eleanor.

"You should have minded your own business you old ninny. Now I'm going to have to kill you, too."

Eleanor's heart skipped a beat as she stared into the eyes of a crazy woman.

Just then, the sound of a police siren filled the air.

Lynda jerked sideways and peered out the window.

Officer Joe Nelson exited his patrol car and raced to the front door, one hand on his gun holster and the other on his baton.

"Tell him you're fine and to leave." Lynda shoved Eleanor toward the front door, the gun pointed at the back of her neck.

The doorbell rang.

Eleanor hovered near the side, the cool tip of the gun firmly pressed against her skin. "Yes?"

"It's Officer Joe Nelson, Eleanor. Is everything okay?"

Eleanor had a split second to decide. No matter what she said, Lynda planned to kill her. At least if the officer attempted to come in, she would have a fighting chance.

"I'm being held hostage!" she yelled through the door.

A piercing pain shot through Eleanor's skull as Lynda Clemson grabbed a fist full of Eleanor's hair and threw her to the floor.

Lynda leveled her gun and fired a shot through the front door, narrowly missing Officer Joe Nelson.

The cop hit the pavement and quickly crawled to the side of the house. He snatched his radio from the hip clip. "This is Officer Joe Nelson. I have a 417 with a possible hostage situation. Requesting immediate backup. The suspect is armed and dangerous."

Eleanor remained motionless on the floor and stared at Lynda Clemson as she backed away from the door.

The woman was out of her mind!

"C'mon granny. We're going out the back way."

Lynda reached down to pull Eleanor to her feet. Eleanor shifted to the side and rolled over onto her knees. "I can get up."

The women marched over to the rear slider and when Lynda realized there was no way out the back, Eleanor was certain the woman would promptly shoot her dead.

Sirens filled the air.

"Sit," Lynda commanded, as she kept one eye on Eleanor and the other out the front window. The street quickly filled with cops and cop cars, their doors flung open and their guns drawn.

Lynda began to pace the floor, mumbling under her breath.

Eleanor could only hear a word or two – "murder," "hostage" and "shoot my way out."

Eleanor's eyes darted around the room. She had two choices. Wait to die, or find some way to catch Lynda off guard.

She stiffened her back. Only God was going to take Eleanor Whittaker out! Not some two-bit floozy who had killed her lover!

The only thing within reach was a toaster. She could bonk the woman over the head, but chances were she wouldn't get her good enough to knock her out and grab the gun.

The only other thing on the table and within reach was a plate of cookies. Next to the table was her walker.

"Lynda Clemson, surrender before anyone else gets hurt." Officer Joe Nelson's voice echoed through a bullhorn. "We have the place surrounded. There's no way out."

Lynda paused her pacing as she counted. "Six...make that seven cop cars!"

Eleanor shifted to her feet and reached for her walker.

Lynda gave her a brief sideways glance. Deeming Eleanor a non-threat, she turned her attention to the front of the house again.

Eleanor seized her chance while Lynda's attention focused on the police. She tightened her grip on the walker, lifted it up in front of her, tilted it sideways and charged at Lynda Clemson like a bull.

One of the front walker wheels made contact with the back of Lynda's head. The other wheel jabbed her in the middle of the back.

"Ugh!" Lynda stumbled forward and Eleanor continued her assault. The woman, caught off guard, dropped to her knees and fell forward. During the fall, Lynda lost her grip on the gun, which landed a few feet away.

Eleanor, seizing her opportunity, trampled over the top of Lynda and darted to the front door. She shoved the chair aside, jerked the door open and darted out onto her porch.

The first thing Eleanor saw were guns, pointed right at her. She lifted her hands. "Don't shoot!"

She eased down the steps and over to Officer Joe Nelson, who placed a protective arm around her shoulders and swiftly pulled her to safety behind his open patrol car door.

The next several moments were a blur of activity as an officer tossed a container of tear gas through the open front door.

Moments later, Lynda Clemson crawled out the front door. Police quickly pinned her to the ground and cuffed her.

The realization of all that had occurred hit Eleanor Whittaker like a ton of bricks. Her front yard began to spin and her ears began to ring. The last thing she saw before she fainted was Gloria Rutherford-Kennedy's concerned face.

***

The girls settled into the center table at Dot's Restaurant and waited for Eleanor to tell her tale.

"So before I could stop to think about it, I lifted my walker and charged Lynda Clemson, knocking her over and then running out the front door of my house." Eleanor lifted the teacup to her lips and sipped.

"What an incredible story," Lucy said as she reached for a pecan swirl and nibbled the edge.

Ruth, who knew all the goings-on in the town of Belhaven, chimed in. "The story goes that Ed Mueller was planning to rendezvous at Lynda Clemson's cottage the night of his death. Before he went there, he stopped by the Quik Stop to buy a bottle of wine and some deli items, along with cleaning supplies."

"Wining and dining his girlfriend," Margaret said.

Ruth nodded. "Yeah. Well, apparently he began to hit on Sally Keane and when she gave him the cold shoulder, he finally got the hint and left."

"Lynda Clemson stopped by the store a short time after Ed had left and Sally told Lynda how Ed had just been there and hit on her."

"Enraged, Lynda left the store after getting into it with Sally. She showed up on Ed's cottage doorstep and they argued inside after she confronted him about flirting with Sally. They got into a physical altercation and Ed slapped her face. Lynda stormed out."

Ruth continued. "Ed followed her to her cottage and the argument escalated. Lynda grabbed an ice pick and stabbed him, later claiming she didn't want to kill him. Realizing he was dead, she panicked and placed his body on a sled in her shed, dragged his body to the shanty he'd put on the lake and dumped him inside."

Gloria cut in. "I don't understand why he would put his shanty out on the ice if he didn't plan to stay."

"Sheryl told police that was one of the reasons he was there. He put it out on the lake because he planned to sell it."

Gloria remembered the "For Sale" sign under the bag that contained a new lockset. That made sense.

Andrea chimed in. "Sally Keane told Officer Joe Nelson that Ed had hit on her and he confronted him out in front of the Quik Stop before Lynda caught up with him. The next day, after his body was discovered the cop / boyfriend, thinking perhaps Sally had killed him, tried to look for evidence. That was why he was hanging around the Mueller cottage."

"Yep." Ruth confirmed. "When police began questioning Kate Edelson and Eleanor, Lynda vowed to silence them. From her confession, which I heard secondhand from Judith Arnett, who heard it from her cousin, Minnie, who works in dispatch at Montbay County Sheriff's station, she planned to kill Eleanor next and finally Kate."

"Whew!" Gloria shook her head. "Another reason not to go messing around with someone else's husband."

"What about Sally's nametag that we found inside Ed Mueller's cottage?" Gloria thought about the new lockset. "Ed must have planned to change the locks on the doors that night. Maybe he intended to end the relationship, kind of let Lynda down gently."

"Well, that plan backfired," Ruth said. "Apparently, Lynda found Sally's nametag sitting next to the cash register at the Quik Stop and saw the perfect opportunity to set Sally up to take the fall. She put it in the garbage and then placed an anonymous call to the police department, telling them there was evidence inside Mueller's cottage."

Gloria picked up. "Which is why Officer Joe Nelson had gone back to the place again…to look around."

"The only thing is, he didn't bother checking the trash," Andrea chimed in.

"The police sure showed up fast to Eleanor's house," Margaret remarked.

"That's because Officer Joe Nelson was on his way to Lynda Clemson's cottage when he got the call. He and two other officers were right behind him in another patrol car."

Dot touched Eleanor's hand. "Do you need someone to repair your front door?"

Eleanor shook her head. "No. Brian was kind enough to stop by right after it happened. He put a brand new door on and it even latches like it should. I could never get the old one to catch the first time."

Gloria reached for the bag of potatoes, carrots and turnips on the table. "We better start our rounds for the shut-ins," she said.

Lucy hopped out of her chair. "If you want, Eleanor, we can drop you off at home before starting our visits, right Ruth?"

Ruth was their designated driver for the Sunday afternoon visits. "You got it!"

Gloria reached for her crutches and nodded to Dot. "Paul and I will be back later for dinner."

Dot's friends from South Georgia, Rose and Johnnie Morris, had arrived the night before and were coming into the restaurant later that day to have a look around and to meet some of Dot and Ray's friends.

Dot rubbed her hands together. "I can't wait for you to meet them," she said. "All of you!"

Ruth dropped Eleanor off at her place, with a promise from Gloria to check on her the next day.

Al Dickerson was first on the list of shut-ins, having developed pneumonia. Just to be on the safe side, the girls visited him briefly from the doorway and gave him a bag of vegetables they had gathered from their winter stash, along with a container of chicken noodle soup Dot had sent with them.

Their final visit was to George and Maxine Ford. Maxine was doing much better although the two rarely went out, except for doctors' appointments. The girls visited at length and were glad they had spent some time with the couple.

Ruth dropped the girls off in front of Dot's and Gloria headed home to clean up and spend some time with Paul before they returned to the restaurant for dinner.

The afternoon passed quickly. Gloria talked to Jill briefly, who told her they had researched the old coins they'd found in the barn. Although they weren't worth any money, they were old and the boys planned to take them to school for show and tell.

Gloria played on the computer for a while and her stomach began to grumble. She glanced at the clock in the corner of her laptop. "You want to head down to Dot's?" she hollered into the living room where Paul was watching a baseball game.

"Yeah. We can leave whenever you're ready."

She hobbled to the kitchen and let Mally out for a run before they left.

The restaurant wasn't that busy and there were plenty of parking spots in front of the restaurant. Paul pulled into the nearest one, right next to Lucy's yellow jeep and on the other side, Margaret and Don's SUV.

She could see the girls through the front window as they stood off in the corner talking to Dot and Ray and another couple.

Paul waited on the sidewalk for Gloria to catch up. He held the door and Gloria hopped inside.

Dot turned, a huge grin on her face as she waved Paul and Gloria to the back. The Garden Girls and their guests gathered around two new faces.

When they got close, Dot turned to the woman standing next to her. "Rose, this is my dear friend, Gloria and her new husband, Paul."

Gloria balanced on one leg and held out her hand. The woman grasped her hand and leaned forward to hug her. "My goodness sakes! This is the infamous super sleuth Gloria!"

Dot turned to the man. "This is Rose's husband, Johnnie."

Two kind, brown eyes met Gloria's and the edges crinkled up as Johnnie smiled. "Nice to meet you both," he said with a touch of Southern twang.

Gloria, proud of her keen sense of judgment, instantly liked the two. They were good people. Hopefully, they would like what they saw and stick around.

She shook his hand. "And I have heard so much from Dot and Ray about you. We hope you get a good look around and decide to make this home."

Rose crossed her arms over her ample bosom. "This is a charming town. We would like to do a little more looking around, but so far, we like what we see. Dot needs to be taking a little more time off. Johnnie and I need to stay a little busier."

She flashed a grin. "Course we may have to bring a little more Southern cookin' to the menu," she teased. "Y'all ever had grits and eggs?"

Gloria hadn't, but they sounded intriguing. She rubbed her hands together. "I can hardly wait."

Rose pointed at Gloria's cast. "What in heavens name happened to you?"

Dot rolled her eyes.

Paul chuckled.

Gloria gave them both a dark stare. "I-uh, was chasing after a peeping tom, fell into a gopher tortoise hole and broke my leg."

"On her honeymoon," Dot added.

"Lawd have mercy!" Rose turned to Dot. "I can't wait to hear all about your girls' adventures!"

Ruth and Andrea arrived and crowded around the newcomers.

Paul and Gloria made their way to an empty table and settled in. Paul picked up the menu and then nodded at Rose and Ruth, who were talking animatedly and pointing in their direction. "Looks like Rose and Johnnie are getting the lowdown on the infamous Gloria Rutherford-Kennedy," he chuckled.

"Hmm." Gloria picked up the menu and pretended to study the items, although she knew the menu by heart. "I hope they don't get the wrong impression," she sniffed.

"Oh, I doubt that," Paul said.

Ray excused himself from the group and approached Paul and Gloria's table, glasses of ice water in hand. "You two know what you want?"

"The special," Gloria said. "Meatloaf, mashed potatoes and green beans."

"Ditto." Paul dropped the menu in the center slot. "I hope this works out with the Morris's."

"Me too." Ray jotted down their order and tapped the tip of the pen on top of the order pad. "If Rose and Johnnie decide to stay and become partners, this will be an answer to prayer."

Gloria swirled the straw around in her glass. "I have been praying," she simply said.

After dinner and saying their good-byes to everyone, Paul and Gloria made their way out of the restaurant and onto the sidewalk.

Gloria tugged on the zipper of her winter coat. "This has been a crazy week. I'm ready to go home and snuggle up with my better half."

"Me too," Paul agreed. "Say, you wouldn't happen to remember where you put that container of hot spices Alice sent over the other day? I'm craving a dish of spicy salsa!"

The end.

The Series Continues... Book 13 Coming Soon!

If you enjoyed reading "Look Into My Ice", please take a moment to leave a review. It would be greatly appreciated! Thank you!

Get Free Books and More!

Sign up for my Free Cozy Mysteries Newsletter to get free and discounted books, giveaways & soon-to-be-released books!

hopecallaghan.com/newsletter/

"Stick to your ribs" Goulash

<u>Ingredients</u>

1 lb lean ground beef (can sub ground chicken or ground turkey)
1 large yellow onion, chopped
6 cloves garlic, chopped
3 cups water
1 (15 oz) can tomato sauce
1 (14.5 oz) can diced tomatoes-including juice
1 large green pepper, chopped
1 (6 oz) can tomato paste
2 tablespoons Italian herb seasoning
¼ teaspoon black pepper
1 teaspoon sugar
2 cups uncooked elbow macaroni (or shells)
2 tablespoons salt (add additional salt to taste)

<u>Directions</u>
In large Dutch oven or large saucepan, cook and stir the ground beef over medium-high heat, until brown (about 10 mins).

Skim off excess fat. Stir in onion, garlic and green pepper. Cook and stir the meat mixture until the onions are translucent, about 10 more minutes. (Make sure the garlic doesn't burn)

Stir in water, tomato sauce, diced tomatoes, tomato

paste, Italian seasoning, salt, sugar and pepper (everything else except the pasta).

Bring mixture to boil over medium heat. Reduce heat to low. Stir in pasta. Cover and simmer over low heat until pasta is tender, stirring occasionally. (About 20 minutes.) Remove from heat.

*If you substitute ground chicken or ground turkey, add a small amount of vegetable or olive oil (approx. 2 tablespoons) to brown the meat, then stir in pepper, onion and garlic so that it doesn't stick.

Made in the USA
Monee, IL
28 December 2020